Through
the Small Door

Enjoy the magic of reading.

Zanne Serig

Zanne Serig

Bloomington, IN  Milton Keynes, UK

AuthorHouse™
1663 Liberty Drive, Suite 200
Bloomington, IN 47403
www.authorhouse.com
Phone: 1-800-839-8640

AuthorHouse™ UK Ltd.
500 Avebury Boulevard
Central Milton Keynes, MK9 2BE
www.authorhouse.co.uk
Phone: 08001974150

© 2006 Zanne Serig. All rights reserved.

No part of this book may be reproduced, stored in a retrieval system, or transmitted by any means without the written permission of the author.

First published by AuthorHouse 4/26/2006

ISBN: 1-4259-2515-4 (sc)

Library of Congress Control Number: 2006902341

Printed in the United States of America
Bloomington, Indiana

This book is printed on acid-free paper.

This book is dedicated to the 2004-2005 seventh grade Panthers at Windsor Middle School in Windsor, Virginia, and to their science teacher who inspired the character of Mrs. Lawrence.

Acknowledgements

A special thank you goes to Cathy Palmer and JJ Stephens for their continued support, advice, and suggestions in preparing this book.

I would also like to thank Jennifer Mustoe for her suggestions and advice.

1
Secrets

I never expected that one day I'd move my dresser and behind it I would find a small doorknob connected to a rickety wooden door three feet tall. Who would have thought when Aunt Kate had volunteered to help me rearrange my furniture that I would make such a startling and puzzling discovery? The knob, brass with a few dents in it, shone brightly in the dim light cast by my bedside lamp. I gasped when I saw the door and Kate turned toward me. "Did you hurt yourself moving that dresser alone?"

Wanting to know if she saw the door too, I replied, "No, but I dropped my bracelet back here and now I can't find it."

"Let me look," she offered as she joined me behind the dresser. She knelt down and felt around on the floor without success. She stood and pushed her glasses back up on her nose with the index finger of her right hand. "It's not here, Sam. Are you sure this is where you lost it?"

"Well, I'm not absolutely sure, but I can't think where else it could be," I answered her as she moved back to the desk.

She hadn't seemed to notice the door. Maybe I had imagined it. I looked again and there it was, right where I had first seen it. Aunt Kate said nothing about a door. I guess she didn't see it. I left the dresser sitting out from the wall while I got the broom and swept behind it. I had almost finished sweeping when I heard Uncle Art calling up the stairs.

"Kate, let's go get a video for this evening."

"Do you need my help moving this furniture or can you manage until I get back?" Aunt Kate asked.

I was anxious to check out the small door so I urged her to go with Uncle Art. "We both know the kinds of movies he picks. You'd better go with him and make sure he gets somethin' interestin' instead of one of those old westerns he loves so much. I'll be fine. In fact I'll finish sweepin' and wait for you before I move the bed."

She smiled at me as she responded to her husband. "I'll be there in a minute, dear." Turning back to me she questioned, "Are you sure?"

I laughed, "Go get us a good movie."

Aunt Kate left the room and I wanted to run straight to the little door. Instead, I waited until I heard Uncle Art's car start and rattle away down the street.

I rushed back to the dresser and looked behind it again. No, it wasn't my imagination. The doorknob gleamed in the lamplight, and as I grasped the dented brass doorknob, a strange tingling sensation started at my fingertips and traveled up my arm as fast as a race car driver taking the checkered flag. Curiosity got the better of me, and I gave the knob a spontaneous twist. With a strange crack, the doorknob turned and I pushed the door. The hinges creaked eerily as the door slowly swung toward me. I must admit, my stomach felt all funny like the time I ate too much spaghetti and puked it up an hour later. Why was there a door behind my dresser? What was on the other side of the door? If I went through the opening, would I be able to return? I stooped down and scrunched through hesitantly, amazed by what I saw. It was every kid's dream and every parent's nightmare. Obviously, I had entered a garden. However, this was no ordinary garden. The grass looked like the sparkly green sprinkles I put on ice cream. The trees had twisted black licorice for trunks and smaller twisted licorice limbs, with red and yellow gumdrop leaves. My mouth watered and my stomach growled softly. The fluffy cotton candy clouds with gigantic paper cones sticking out every few feet drifted lazily across the rapidly darkening sky, reflecting the pinkish light from the setting sun. All around me, I could see candy in bushes, candy in trees, and candy covering the ground.

Suddenly a movement in the licorice tree caught my eye as something or someone swung through the colorful gumdrops high above the ground. When I looked closely, I saw that the swinger was a gingerbread man holding tightly to a rope made of taffy. He dropped lightly to the ground and ran swiftly toward me, his feet crunching across the green sprinkles of grass.

The gingerbread man stopped in front of me as if he was expecting my arrival. "Welcome to the candy garden, Sam." He panted a little as he stopped running and rubbed his sugary brown hands together. His deep baritone voice sounded almost like my Uncle Art's. Funny, my Uncle Art's favorite food is gingerbread, I thought.

"Did you just say somethin'? What is goin' on here? Gingerbread men don't swing through trees or talk." I stooped down to look him in his sparkly brown frosted eyes.

He returned my gaze without blinking. "I know your mom taught you better manners than that, Sam. However, I'll forgive your rudeness this time." He ended our staring contest by reaching out and touching my cheek with his cookie hand. "What do you think of the garden, Sam?"

"I've never seen a garden like this." I could feel my mouth watering at the thought of all that delicious candy. "What grows here besides licorice and gumdrop trees? And how do you know my name?"

"I see you're curious. That's good," the gingerbread man responded while removing a green and white peppermint from his cookie pocket. He handed it to me and watched with a sparkle in his chocolate frosting eyes as I popped it in my mouth.

"This doesn't taste like peppermint," I said after I had sucked on the candy for a minute, savoring the flavor. "It tastes like chocolate cake," I told him, licking my lips.

"And the red and white candies," he chuckled, watching my face, "taste like strawberry shortcake." The laugh lines at the corners of his brown frosting eyes smoothed out as suddenly he stopped smiling. "Now, I'll give you some answers. Yes, this is a candy garden, which doesn't always look like this. It really isn't my garden, but yours. What you see here reflects what you are and what you will become. The fact that it now looks like a candy shop tells me that you are a sweet girl with a sweet tooth. Each plant tells me more about you."

"How can you know anythin' about me by lookin' at the plants?"

"Stop asking more questions until after I answer your original ones." His round frosting eyes gazed at me seriously for a moment. "Hmm, where were we? Oh, yes. What grows in this garden?" He beckoned with a sugar-tipped finger for me to follow him. We began to stroll slowly through the candy garden, my feet crunching along the green sprinkles. "See that large orange flower? That is a curiosity flower." I found myself looking in the direction he pointed. The flower had a strange elongated wedge shape, and sprinkles of a white crystal substance covered the orange jellied petals.

By now, the sun had set completely, and I could no longer see the soft cotton candy clouds. An eerie yellowish glow, which seemed to come from the candy plants in the unusual garden, cast a faint light around us as we continued our leisurely stroll around the garden on a winding path of multicolored taffy. Before long, the gingerbread man stopped in front of a tall plant with long stems and a dozen blue and green candy-coated buds about the size of a dime.

"What grows on this one?" I couldn't resist asking.

"Oh, this is an understanding stalk. You'll notice that the buds haven't opened fully yet. But they will soon, very soon." His baritone voice shook with laughter as he answered.

"How soon? Will I get to see them?"

His laughter echoed around the garden. "Of course, you'll get to see them, since they're yours."

"Mine?" His smile broadened as one of the green buds started opening. "Oh! I understand. The garden is

mine, so when I understand somethin', the buds open."
I could feel my grin growing to match the one on the gingerbread man's face. "This is kinda fun. What else can I find in my garden?"

"Come on, and I'll show you."

A little further along the winding path, the gingerbread man paused, reached out and plucked a lemon drop, which he placed in my right hand. "This is the intelligence bed. As you can see, there is no shortage here." His brilliant smile lit his round cookie face.

"Some strange things grow in this garden," I told him while I examined the lemon drop carefully before popping it in my mouth. It tasted a little sour after the green and white peppermint candy and made my lips pucker.

"Strange? Perhaps you're right. Nevertheless, the garden grows itself. You've seen the curiosity, understanding, and intelligence plants. In addition, there are trustworthiness, sincerity, and common sense. Today, if you look carefully, you can also find a few bushes of honesty, impatience, stubbornness, and determination." Each time he mentioned another quality, he pointed to a different candy plant. He pointed out candy canes, butterscotch candies, chocolate cream drops, after dinner mints, jellybeans, caramels, and gumballs. Scattered among the other kinds of candy, I could see candy corn peeking through. The candy corn was so plentiful that I thought it must represent the weeds in this otherwise perfect garden. He took my hand and led me to a section of the garden that looked like freshly made fudge and I had to resist the temptation to reach out and sample it. The gingerbread man added, "We mustn't forget the magic." He pointed to the fudge. "No, it wouldn't do at all to leave out the magic." The pink sugar frosted mouth twitched with just the hint of a smile as he pronounced his last words.

"Magic?" This was my garden and magic was growing in it. How was that possible? My stomach felt like it does whenever the teacher calls on me and I don't know the answer.

"No interruptions, young lady," the gingerbread man chuckled as he sensed my impatience.

"But…" I began.

"It looks like I was right about the impatience," he added, almost under his breath as he cut me off before I could speak again.

The gingerbread man rubbed his hands together. "Let's get back to your questions. How do I know your name? Sam, I've known your name since the day of your birth. Your full name is Samantha Anne Laurence, isn't it?"

My mouth dropped open in disbelief. Who was this gingerbread man? How did he know me?

"More questions, Sam?" he nodded as if he had read my mind and heard my unspoken thoughts. "You'll find out who I am when the time is right, and not before. No, Sam," he continued as I opened my mouth to ask something else. "I won't tell you when that will be."

"I know you said no more questions, but I just gotta know about the door behind my dresser. How long has it been there? Why haven't I seen it before now? Does anyone else know about it? Am I imaginin' all this, or is it real?"

"My, you are the curious one, all right. Last question first," the gingerbread man replied as he thoughtfully rubbed his smooth chin with one cookie hand. Sugar dusted off his hand and fell to the sparkly ground. "Imagination fuels the world. Reality is just imagination brought to life. The two together create the world as we know it." He paused as he tilted his cookie head to one side and regarded me solemnly. "Does that tell you what you want to know, Sam?"

I could feel the frown pulling at the corners of my mouth. "Not really," I answered after the slightest hesitation.

"I appreciate your honesty, Sam. Right now, I can't explain everything to you. That's not my job. More than that, I am not at liberty to tell you. Soon you will learn a secret that I have kept for many decades. What you do with that knowledge, once it is yours, will be up to you."

I shuffled my feet uneasily, shifting my weight from one foot to the other and caught myself absentmindedly twisting a strand of my long reddish-brown hair.

"Relax, Sam. I won't force any truths on you that you can't handle, nor will I tell you to trust me. You don't really know me, so how can I expect you to do that?" All this serious talk coming from a cookie man seemed weird and I giggled to cover my nervousness.

"You haven't answered my questions about the door behind my dresser." I twirled a strand of hair around my fingers.

"You don't miss much, do you, Sam?" The small smile grew into a huge grin that spread across the brown cookie face. "The small door in your bedroom appeared on your seventh birthday. Discovering the door shows that you are ready to learn my secret. You have reached the age of understanding." He paused to pluck a purple candy blossom from a large untrimmed bush near the licorice tree. He gently placed the bloom behind my left ear before continuing, which I thought was sweet. I had never before received a flower from anyone, especially a talking gingerbread man. "I may be the one to reveal that secret to you or maybe not. However, I can tell you that you must trust the one who makes the revelation to you. You must also promise never to remove that brass doorknob. Only special people can see the door, so don't worry about your mom finding it."

"I don't understan'," I protested.

"Don't worry about that now. You will understand soon, I promise you. Now I need to get you back to your home before someone realizes that you're not there." A sad look crossed the cookie face at the mention of my departure. I thought I saw a tear forming, like a drop of watery frosting, trembling and waiting to fall. The gingerbread man tried to hide his emotion by quickly swiping his doughy hand across his eyes.

"What's wrong?"

"Nothing is wrong," he answered gruffly, his words catching in his throat. "I will miss you, that's all. You brought sunshine into my day."

"Will I ever see you again?" I could feel the sting of tears starting to form in my own eyes, too.

He swallowed quickly and rubbed his round brown eyes again. "Sure, you'll see me again, maybe sooner than you expect, although I may not appear to you again as a gingerbread man, or maybe I will." He rubbed his doughy hands together while he enjoyed his own joke.

"The next time I see you; will I know this secret that you talked about?"

"Probably not," he said with a chuckle. "But it won't be long before you learn the truth."

The light had almost disappeared, and the gingerbread man nervously began pacing back and forth under the licorice and gumdrop tree. He bent forward slightly, his fingers laced behind his cookie back. He stopped pacing, turned to face me and said, "I know a lot about you, Sam. But there is one more thing that I need to know before you go."

"What?"

"Are you reliable?" he asked me, his eyes watching my face.

"Of course, I'm reliable," I replied with a grin that spread from ear to ear.

"Then I can depend on you?" Though his face still looked brown and doughy, for some reason, I could tell that something was bothering him. Maybe it was his frosting eyes, which drooped as he frowned at me.

"Depend on me to do what?" I asked hesitantly while cookie crumbs fell from his face as he continued to frown.

"Be patient and I'll tell you," he said. "Come with me," he added as he placed his soft smooth cookie hands on my shoulders.

He steered me back to the small door I had used earlier to enter the candy garden. He turned to me and said in a whisper, so low I barely heard him, "Can you keep a secret?"

"Sure," I whispered back, knowing that a secret was safe with me for about a day.

"When you go back through that door, you won't be the same as you were before." He flashed a crooked sugary smile at me.

"Before what?"

"Before you came to visit me," the gingerbread man responded as he pushed me closer to the small door.

"I won't? How will I be different?" I asked him.

"I can't tell you," he replied as his smile disappeared, and he grasped the dented brass doorknob.

"Why not?" I asked him.

"Because I can keep a secret, too," he laughed as he pushed me gently through the door into my own bedroom.

2
Vanished

It was quiet and dark when I stepped back through the small door and felt a gentle puff of air as it closed behind me. I usually left the stereo in my bedroom blasting, but now the silence engulfed me, like someone had stuffed cotton in my ears. I also knew that I had left the bedroom light on when I had embarked on my unexpected adventure. I could remember the glint of the lamplight on the dented doorknob. Now there was no music and no bedside light. I shoved the dresser to the wall to hide the door and its dented brass knob. As I moved the dresser, I felt the candy blossom fall from my hair to my shoulders. I retrieved it and stuffed the sugary purple blossom into the pocket of my jeans. Memories of what had just happened filled my mind as I remembered the weird candy garden and all of the strange and delightful plants I had seen. Had I really talked to a gingerbread man? Was there really a small door behind my dresser? Nah, couldn't be. Maybe I should check just to make sure. No, if I start looking for doors behind dressers, I will be crazy. It was just a dream, that's all it was. Things like that just don't happen. I had better write this crazy dream in my diary while I can still remember it. Maybe I can use some of it in a story for English class. That would make a great story! Yeah, I'll write it down now before I forget it like I do most of my dreams.

Suddenly, I realized I had been standing there in the dark thinking crazy thoughts. Maybe I needed to turn on the light before I really went off the deep end, as Uncle Art would say. I felt my way across the familiar room to my bedside table. I turned the little knob on the lamp, but it wouldn't come on. I opened the drawer of the table to find the flashlight my mom made me keep there. As I felt around for it, my groping fingers encountered my diary and a crinkly piece of paper. I took them out and tossed them on my bed to get them out of the way while I continued my search.

Without warning, a bright beam of greenish light shot from behind the dresser and illuminated the items I had placed on my bed. The creamy white cover on my diary now had a greenish tint to it, but what held my attention was the paper I had removed with the diary. It was a drawing that had started to curl around the edges. It wasn't really the paper, but the image on it, which had my attention. In the beam from the bright light, I could see a huge distorted blue blob that resembled a face. What could this be? Why would I keep a drawing of a blue face? Now I knew I was going crazy.

The greenish light shifted to the right just as a tiny voice, which seemed to come from the mysterious beam, exclaimed, "There you are! I've been waiting for you. Where were you?"

"What do you mean, where was I? I haven't been anywhere." I squinted and peered into the light, trying to locate the speaker. "Who are you and why are you in my room? Where did you come from? Are you part of this weird dream I must be havin'?"

"Look around you," the tiny voice continued. "All of this is real. It isn't a dream, and it's far from over."

"Sure it's a dream," I argued with the voice while peering behind the dresser to see who had spoken. "Candy gardens don't exist, and everyone knows that gingerbread men are just cookies and can't talk. Every bit of this is a dream, even you." I looked under the dresser, still trying to find the owner of the voice.

"Are you sure about that?" the teeny voice went on as I paused for breath. "Are you even sure that this IS your room? Do *you* even exist?"

"Are you crazy? Of course, I'm sure. Whose room could it be if it isn't mine? Of course, I exist. I'm standin' here talkin' to you, aren't I?" What was wrong with me? Why was I talking to a voice coming from a light beam? I had taken about all of this that I could.

I used the glowing light to find my way to my bedside and turned the knob on the lamp again. Why wouldn't the light come on?

The voice went on, sounding even squeakier. "Your room needed extensive repairs after the pecan tree crashed into the roof during the hurricane two years ago. You were in your room when the tree fell, but your parents couldn't find you when they cleaned up the mess. They never even found your body. You vanished off the face of the earth."

"Wait a minute, I remember when that tree fell." I interrupted. "Are you tellin' me I died two years ago when it came through the roof?"

"Only time will tell," the voice replied.

"Why are you doin' this to me? This is *my* room. These are *my* clothes, *my* shoes, all *my* softball trophies, *my* stamp collection, and *my* jigsaw puzzles." The words almost tripped over each other as fear and worry crept up my spine. My fingers started tingling, and I felt faint. Could this mysterious voice be right? I recalled the hurricane and remembered the tree hitting the roof of my bedroom. Had I died, and wouldn't I know if I had? Of course not, silly. How could a dead person know anything?

Although I hadn't spoken my doubts aloud, the voice cut me off. "Whoa! Slow down! One thing at a time," the tiny voice interrupted before any more questions could form. "This is your room, or would have been, if you had survived. Your parents had the repairs made and put everything back like it had been. Your mom never gives up on finding you and keeps praying for your return."

I couldn't stand it any longer. I blurted out, "If I'm dead, how can I be talkin' to you? Where have I been for the last two years? Why is the house so quiet?" I could feel the tingling in my fingers grow stronger as I waited for the answers.

"Gottcha!" the tiny voice squeaked, breathless with laughter. "I always wanted to tell someone that they didn't exist any more. You should have seen your face. I think you turned as green as this light that accompanies me everywhere."

"That wasn't very nice of you." Anger toward the voice for playing such a cruel joke on me made my voice tremble.

"Nice? No. Fun? Yes." The voice seemed fainter than before.

"You still haven't told me who you are or why you're in my room." If I could have gotten my hands on the owner of that little voice, I would have choked out the truth.

The faint voice responded, "I am the keeper of the doors that lead to parallel worlds. The gingerbread man sent me to see that you made it home safely. He worries about you all the time, especially when your parents travel for your dad's business. Of course, this time it's their anniversary cruise, but even so, he still worries about you. Your Uncle Art and Aunt Kate went to rent a video and should be back shortly. Oh, yes, I forgot to tell you, the electricity won't work while I'm here because I drain the power. I do like this green glow, don't you? Now, Miss Inquisitive, what else do you need to know?"

My anger slowly faded away as I realized that the voice had told the truth. My parents had taken a cruise for their anniversary. I remembered telling them goodbye yesterday morning. Uncle Art and his wife Kate, who had no children of their own, always jumped at a chance to stay with me and spoil me rotten when my parents traveled.

The voice had given me a chance to ask questions, and I didn't want to throw away that opportunity. Therefore, I quickly asked, "Who is the gingerbread man? Why does he worry about me? Why is there a door behind my dresser?" I could have gone on indefinitely, but the rapidly fading voice stopped me.

"You ask more questions than anyone else I have ever met. I don't have much time left, so let me put my answers this way:

The gingerbread man is your friend.
On him, you can always depend.
Call on him when you're in trouble,
And he will respond on the double.
The door is simply a portal
That isn't accessible to any mortal.
Your other questions will have to wait,
But some of the credit goes to Kate."

I was still puzzling over the rhyme when another question occurred to me. "What do you mean the door can't be used by a mortal? I used it, didn't I?"

This time there was no answering voice. Only silence. The beam of light flashed like a firefly on a summer evening, getting dimmer as it faded out, leaving me in the dark in the middle of my bedroom. I started toward the door as my stereo began playing and the bedside lamp turned on by itself.

3
Chills

When the lights came on, I caught a glimpse of my reflection in the mirror on my dresser. I did a double take when I realized that the strange distorted face looking back at me was my own. I touched my face and the electric blue face with yellow warts on it in the mirror had my hands on it, too! I pulled the strands of long stringy purple hair then let it plop back to my shoulders. A sudden chill ran down my spine. Could that face belong to me?

I rushed into the bathroom to look in that mirror. It, too, showed the reflection of some monster escaped from a coloring book. Quickly I dashed warm water onto my blueness and patted it dry with a fluffy towel. I kept my face in the towel for a moment while I held my breath. Slowly, I pulled the towel off my face so I could look in the mirror again. I was still electric blue, and the yellow warts seemed to have mushroomed into miniature hills on my face. I wanted to cry but was afraid the tears would be tomato juice or tropical punch. Maybe my face was a mask and if I scratched it, it would peel off, but as I picked at the skin, I knew it was no mask. What could I do? I avoided the mirror. My face was pure ugly.

Think, Sam, I thought. Maybe some of the cold cream Mom used to remove makeup would help. I ran to Mom's room and pawed through the assorted jars and bottles on her dresser. I couldn't find the small pink jar. Mom must have taken it with her. I would have to try something else. But what?

I looked up and saw that hideous blue face staring back at me. Three mirrors couldn't be wrong, could they? However, the gingerbread man was right. I definitely hadn't looked like this before my visit to the candy garden. What had happened to my straight white teeth, my lovely brown eyes, and dull reddish-brown hair? If I get my limp, straight hair back, I'll never pester Mom about getting a perm again, I thought. I started twisting a strand of purple hair between my fingers. Then I caught myself picking at the huge ugly wart on the tip of my nose. Gross! This couldn't be me, could it?

A talking gingerbread man, a voice coming from a beam of light… and, now this! Mom, where are you when I need you?

I galloped down the stairs, taking the steps two at a time. I reached the large entryway at the same time Gumby, my temperamental black cat, entered it from the dining area. I knew when he first got a good look at me because his back arched like a Halloween cat. His tail fluffed up to three times its normal size as he hissed, and sprang for my face. I raised my arms to block his assault, getting a couple of scratches on my forearms. Gumby hit the floor running and zipped up the stairs so fast he was a blur of black fur. Poor Gumby! Poor me! This was too much. I needed someone to help me. From somewhere upstairs, I heard a muffled shriek like someone scraping his fingernails along a blackboard.

I whirled and ran from the house, across the street to my best friend, Carl's. We'd been buddies since his family moved in when I was four and Carl was five.

Carl knew everything. He would be able to help me. I rang Carl's doorbell and shivered as another chill ran down my spine. I had the creepy feeling that someone was watching me. No one answered, so I rang the bell again. I tapped on the door impatiently. Finally, I gave up and turned toward the street.

The feeling that someone was watching me wouldn't go away. I didn't see anyone on the street, so I thought I had imagined it. My teeth started chattering, and I realized that I had left my house without grabbing my jacket. That would solve my problem, all right. Freeze to death and it wouldn't matter what I looked like. I returned to my house to get my jacket and scribbled a quick note to my aunt and uncle telling them I had gone to Jasmine's. I didn't want them worrying about me, and I sure didn't want them seeing me when I looked like this.

I pulled my jacket on with the hood drawn tightly around my face. Keeping my head down, I began my quest for Carl.

A jumble of thoughts ran through my mind as I jogged down the sidewalk in front of my house. Where could Carl have gone? Think, Sam, think! It's a nice evening, and the city put those new lights in at the skateboard park. Maybe he went there to work on that new move he tried to explain to me. Or maybe he went to the library to finish his research on the planet project Mrs. Lawrence assigned. It IS due Tuesday of next week, and I know Carl hates to wait 'til the last minute for stuff like that. Or maybe, just maybe he went to Ryan's house to help Ryan with his flaky computer. That would be just like Carl. He's so crazy about computers, I'm surprised he doesn't have one with him all the time. That's it. I'll check Ryan's first. But how can I do that? I don't want anyone to see me looking like a clown. How would I explain? C'mon, Sam. Use your brain. I know! I'll call Ryan and ask if Carl is there. Then I won't have to let anybody see what a 'beauty' I've become.

I spun around and ran back to my house, pulling my hood tighter as headlights from a passing vehicle lit the street. I ducked into the shadow of the house until the car turned the corner.

I fumbled with the doorknob, my fingers stiff from the cold. In the living room, I picked up the phone and noticed that my fingers had swollen a little. I punched in Ryan's number, and stood tapping my foot impatiently as the phone rang and rang and rang. So much for that idea. What next?

I left my house again, walking fast, heading for the library, thinking he might be there. I had gone two or three blocks when the hair on my neck stood on end, and goose bumps popped up on my arms. I knew it wasn't the chilly temperatures outside causing my discomfort. Someone was watching me. I kept going and reached the library just as Miss Weaver, the ancient librarian, locked the front door. Another dead end. I ducked down behind a bench and waited for her to leave.

The only other place I could think to look was the skateboard park. By now, the feeling of being watched had grown so strong that I kept glancing back to see if someone was there. I thought I saw a shadow moving near the base of a tree I had just passed. Increasing my pace, I reached the gate to the skateboard park to find it dark and deserted. Where was Carl? In a town this size, there weren't that many places to go on a Friday night.

I broke into a run, my feet pounding against the pavement. I didn't know where to go. I had to find someone who could help me. Someone who could give me some answers. Where was everyone?

4

Can Carl Help?

I heard running feet hitting the sidewalk behind me and whirled around to see Carl barreling frantically toward me. He was breathing heavily and gasping for breath by the time he reached me. I giggled. Carl *never* moved fast in his life unless he was on wheels. Since I wasn't one to look a gift horse in the mouth, I stood and waited patiently for him.

He skidded to a stop in front of me and stood bent over with his hands on his knees, trying to catch his breath. His shaggy light brown hair fell forward hiding his hazel eyes. I heard his breath whistling through his nostrils each time he exhaled. His chest heaved. When he had recovered sufficiently to speak, he exclaimed, "I haven't moved that fast since I stirred up that nest of hornets last fall!" As he straightened up and got his first glimpse of my face in the dim light cast by the streetlamp, he burst out laughing. "Whoa! Is that you, Sam?"

I sighed loudly and rolled my eyes as I answered him. "Yes, Carl, it's me. And don't you dare say anythin'!"

"I can't help it, Sam. You look so… so different!" he sputtered. "What have you done to your hair? Why do you have that awful blue make-up on your face and what in the world happened to your hands? This isn't a dress rehearsal for next Halloween, is it? It's the middle of December, not October." His shoulders shook with suppressed laughter as he continued to study my face.

I glanced down and saw deformed hands that looked nothing like my own. My fingers had ballooned up like sausages. I couldl not let this new development sidetrack me. I really needed Carl's help.

"Carl, I really need your help," I could hear the desperation in my voice.

"You got that right. Look at you! You're a mess," Carl replied. "Know what you look like, Sam?" His grin widened, making the skin around his eyes wrinkle.

"Yeah. I looked in the mirror. Several times. You're enjoyin' this, aren't you, Carl?"

Carl tried, and failed, to erase the grin from his familiar face.

Headlights flashed along the trees as a car turned onto the street. Carl grabbed my shoulders and turned me so that my back was to the street.

"No, silly. I know you looked in a mirror. What I mean is your face and hair remind me of somethin' I've seen before."

"How could you've seen anythin' that looks like this before?" I asked as I pushed the hood back from my face, flipped my hair out of the collar of the jacket and twirled around in front of him to show off the full effect of the mask-like face and purple hair that hung to my waist in limp strands.

"I'm serious, Sam. You remind me of that picture you colored when we were in first grade. You liked it so much that you took it home and taped it to the refrigerator. Remember, Sam? The witch with the yellow warts and blue skin? You loved that picture and had a fit every time your mom wanted to take it down. You showed it off to everyone who came to visit. Remember? Whatever happened to that thing?"

"Mom finally took it down, and I saved it."

"Where did you put it?"

"In the top drawer of my bedside table with my diary." I shrugged. I had almost forgotten about that drawing. That explained the blue picture I had seen in the bedroom earlier.

"Is it still there?" I could tell that Carl was serious. His grin had vanished, and his eyes were narrow slits as he studied my face.

"Yeah. I saw it this afternoon." I frowned as I tried to remember what I had done with the picture. "Why? What does that old drawin' have to do with how I look right now?"

"If I'm right, it could have a lot to do with your, ah, transformation. C'mon, Sam. Let's get that masterpiece of yours, and then we'll get you some help." Carl grabbed one of my twisted hands and began pulling me back toward my house.

Uncle Art's car, a beat-up old convertible, was in the driveway. I pulled back as Carl tried to urge me forward. "Stop it, Carl. I can't go in there lookin' like this."

"Well, you can't stay out here either, and we gotta get that picture."

"Okay, but you wait here. I think I can sneak in without gettin' caught."

Carl snickered softly. "You should be able to. You've done it plenty of times before."

"I have not," I retorted. "Well, maybe once or twice," I admitted as he flashed his toothy grin at me again.

"Hurry," he whispered as a shadow moved across the living room window. "Oh, Sam, try not to let anyone see you." His soft laughter followed me as I sidled around the corner of the house and up the back stairs.

I heard the television in the living room as I snuck up the stairs, making sure to miss the steps that creaked. In my room, Gumby was sleeping on the bed with his front paws resting on the hideous drawing. I tugged gently on the edge of the paper and it slipped free without waking the cat.

With the picture clutched in my sausage-shaped fingers and my heart thudding like a jackhammer in my chest, I crept down the stairs. I held my breath as I inched past the open living room door and tiptoed down the hallway toward the kitchen. I closed the back door behind me and dashed around the side of the house. Carl was waiting for me in the shadow of a large oak tree at the edge of the front yard. I held out the picture and Carl snatched it from me, grabbed my shoulders, and twirled me around so that the light from the front porch shone on my distorted face. Then he held up the drawing I had once cherished as his hazel eyes flickered from the old picture to my distorted face. "Yup, I was right. This thing could be a self portrait." He waved the paper in my face.

Having already looked at the picture carefully in my bedroom and my own hideous face in the mirror, I knew he was right. Apparently, my bizarre looks had a connection to the picture I had colored in first grade.

"Let's go. We're gonna get help for you."

Carl once again grabbed my swollen hand in his strong masculine one and started tugging me down the street. He clutched the picture in his other hand like some kind of lifeline.

"Where are we goin'?" I ducked my head as a truck passed us.

"You'll see when we get there. Wouldn't want to spoil the surprise, now would we?" He lengthened his stride as he continued walking down the street dragging me along. I had to take two steps to every one of his, and if he hadn't been holding onto my hand, I couldn't have kept up. When we had gone several blocks, he turned to me, his chest heaving like fireplace bellows. His eyebrows almost met as he scowled at me. "Sam, you haven't told me what you were doin' to get yourself into this predicament. Start at the beginnin'. Where were you? What were you doin'?"

"If you'll shut your yap for a minute, I'll tell you." Astonished, he stopped walking and stood there in the middle of the sidewalk with his mouth hanging open. I'd never spoken to him like that before. Now that I had his attention, I told him in detail about everything that had happened since I opened the door behind my dresser. I saw a flicker of concern in his hazel eyes when I mentioned finding the door behind my dresser. By the time I got to the part about the tiny voice in the greenish beam of light, he was chewing on his bottom lip as his eyes scrunched up like he had a headache.

When I finished, his mouth still hung open. He was speechless – another first for Carl. His response was just what I had hoped it would be.

"Relax, Sam. We'll figure out what's goin' on." He snapped his fingers. "In fact, I know just what to do." He tugged on my hand again.

"What can we do? Who do you know who can get rid of these?" I gestured wildly at my yellow warts and blue skin.

"You trust me, don't you, Sam?" He grinned at me as he pulled me down the street.

"Of course, I trust you, but you don't have 'ta pull my arm off."

"Sorry. Sometimes I don't know my own strength."

"I bet," I joked, but was grateful when he loosened his death grip.

We walked along silently for several blocks before Carl halted without warning. He stood with his head cocked to one side as if hearing something I couldn't. I wondered with my transformation if I was slowly losing my hearing. The feeling of someone watching me had returned and made me uneasy.

"Let's get outta here." I tugged on his hand this time and shuffled my feet as I waited for Carl to speak. I guess I expected him to joke about my looks again, so he caught me off guard when he turned to me with no hint of a smile. The engaging grin had disappeared. "Sam, no matter what happens tonight, I want you to know that you can depend on me. I'm here for you whenever you need me. I know that sometimes you think of me as an older brother just like I think of you as my little sister. I won't let anything or anyone hurt you."

"Okay, Carl." I answered slowly. "You may be like my big brother, but you're only six months older. What could possibly happen tonight that could hurt me any worse than turning into a first grade blue witch? What more could possibly go wrong?"

"I'm serious, Sam. Things will happen tonight that could change your life."

"What do you mean?"

"I can't tell you even though I want to." Carl's eyes drooped in sadness, and his fists, one of them holding the drawing he had snatched from me, had clenched at his sides.

"Carl, can I ask you somethin'?" Now I wasn't smiling either.

"Sure." He unclenched his fists and laid a hand gently on my shoulder. "What'ya want to know?"

"Do you think someone is watchin' us right now? I have a feelin' that we're bein' followed."

"So, I'm not the only one with that feelin'," he muttered as he peered uneasily into the gloom that surrounded us.

I shook my head a little, while my insides shook a lot.

5

The Machine

The sudden sound of a car backfiring filled the street. Carl and I both jumped. I moved closer to Carl, my heart pounding wildly in my chest. "What now?" I wondered aloud as Carl and I both looked up and down the street. Nothing moved around us.

"Come on!" Carl exclaimed, brushing a lock of his light brown hair from his forehead. "Let's get out of here before somethin' else happens to you." He grabbed one of my twisted hands and began pulling me down the cold, empty street. I had no choice, so I followed, clumping along behind him. We trudged on, and a few minutes later, paused in front of an enormous two-story gray wooden house with shuttered windows. I recognized the place immediately and knew that I never would have imagined this destination. We stood on the sidewalk in front of our science teacher's house. How could Mrs. Lawrence help? What did she know about gingerbread men and blue skin? Why would Carl even think of going to Mrs. Lawrence for help?

Carl rang the doorbell. A disembodied voice wafted from a speaker box above the bell. "How may I help you?"

"Mrs. Lawrence, it's me, Carl."

"Oh, hi, Carl. Kenny isn't here tonight. He and Kristen have gone to visit their uncle in Boston," the voice replied.

"Uh, I didn't come to see Kenny. I need your help with something. Can I come in?" Carl was bouncing up and down on the balls of his feet as he waited for an answer.

"Have you lost your mind?" I whispered. "How can Mrs. Lawrence help me? She's our science teacher, not a magician. Besides, all the kids say she's mean and a real witch. How can she help me?"

Carl glanced back at the street. "You'll see that there's more to Mrs. Lawrence than meets the eye," he whispered back.

"The door's not locked. Come on down to the basement," the voice instructed.

"Thanks, Mrs. Lawrence," Carl replied as he turned the knob, pushed the door open, and before I could protest, dragged me into a well-furnished living room, toward a door in the back wall. "C'mon, Sam. Kenny and I are working on an invention in the basement. Wait'll you see what we've done!"

The Scott twins, Kristen and Kenny were Mrs. Lawrence's foster kids. I knew that Carl had been hanging out with Kenny, who shared his passion for creating new machines and modifying existing ones.

We passed through the rear door into an unlit hallway and scurried down a steep flight of stairs into a spacious, well-lit, black-walled basement room with no windows. In the corner to my right, there was a vat at least four feet deep with clouds of misty steam rising from it and curling along the ceiling. A picture of a black Persian cat sleeping on a red cushion hung on the wall behind the vat.

Carl turned toward the vat, pulling me along. As I stared at the black pot, I could see a vague shape that appeared to be in the mist.

"Hello, Carl, Sam. What's so important that it can't wait until Monday?" The voice belonged to Mrs. Lawrence, my science teacher, but it came from the cloud of vaporous steam.

Where was Mrs. Lawrence? I could hear her, but where was she? What had Carl gotten me into? Didn't I have enough worries without this?

"Where is she?" I whispered, dragging my feet.

"Shh," Carl put his index finger to his lips to shush me.

"Hi, Mrs. Lawrence." Carl answered as he drew me closer to the vat. "Sam seems to have a problem, and I told 'er you could help 'er."

"I see," said the voice. "What can I help you with tonight, young lady? Is Carl giving you a hard time about something? Just let me know, and I'll take care of him." Mrs. Lawrence's voice chuckled. "Oh, I can tell by the look on your face that this is no laughing matter, Carl. Sorry if I seemed to be making light of your situation."

I turned to look at Carl's face. His lips were set in a straight line, and I could see no hint of humor. Carl meant business.

"Can you help Sam?" Carl's voice was serious.

"That depends," came the reply, "on what she needs done."

"Can't you tell by lookin' at her what she needs done?" Carl thrust me toward the vat just as Mrs. Lawrence stepped down and into the light, leaning what looked like a boat paddle against the wall behind her.

"Carl thinks you can help me," I mumbled, pulling my jacket hood tighter around my face.

"Relax, Sam." She reached out and touched the hand that clutched my jacket. "Push your hood back so I can see what has Carl in an uproar."

Slowly I pushed the hood back from my hideous face. Mrs. Lawrence took my chin gently in her hand and turned my face from one side to the other as she gazed at me without smiling. She ran one finger across the wart on the end of my nose. She released my face and turned toward Carl.

"You're right, Carl. Sam has a problem. What do you want me to do?"

"Well, I'd like you to bring back the old Sam. You know, the one with reddish brown hair, human skin without the warts, and hands that don't look like the roots of a cypress tree." Carl turned to look me in the eyes as he added, "Not that you aren't cute the way you are, Sam, in a weird sorta way, but I really like you better when you look like you."

"Why don't you help her, Carl?" Mrs. Lawrence lifted a strand of my lifeless purple hair from my shoulder and rubbed it between her fingers.

Carl's response puzzled me. He hung his head as a small grin tugged at the corner of his mouth. "Well, Mrs. L., I'd help her if I could, but I'm not sure what to do. Besides, I don't think I'm strong enough yet. Please bring back the old Sam." What was Mrs. Lawrence strong enough to do that Carl couldn't?

"All right, Carl." Mrs. Lawrence turned back to me.

"Take your jacket off." My sausage-like fingers fumbled with the zipper tab. I couldn't close my fingers on the tab. Mrs. Lawrence, seeing my predicament, unzipped the jacket for me, and I let it slide off my shoulders into a heap on the floor.

Carl picked up my jacket and tossed it on a table along with his own.

"Tell me how this happened, Sam." Mrs. Lawrence took a small vial from her pocket, removed the top, and standing on tiptoe, poured a thick black molasses-like liquid into the steaming vat.

I drew in a deep breath of air and released it slowly. "Well, I was rearranging my bedroom furniture when I discovered a door behind my dresser. I went through the door into a candy garden and talked to a gingerbread man. He pushed me back into my room after telling me I wouldn't be the same as I was before entering the candy garden." I held my chunky hands up, palms facing my face. "Boy, was he right!"

"Did anything else happen?" Mrs. Lawrence picked up the paddle she had leaned against the wall.

I could feel the wrinkles forming between my eyes as I concentrated. "Oh, yeah. I heard a voice coming from a greenish light. The light shone on my bed, my diary, and an old picture I colored in first grade."

Carl held up the drawing he was clutching. "This picture. I made Sam go back and get it." Carl handed the paper to Mrs. Lawrence. Balancing herself on one foot, she smoothed out the page on her raised knee. She turned the drawing so that the light hit it and studied my ancient artwork.

"That certainly explains your appearance." She held the paper up next to my face and compared the likenesses. "The green light hitting this drawing caused you to change into this image. If the light had hit a picture of a gorilla, that's what you would've become."

I gasped. "You mean it could've been worse?"

"Sure. If the light had hit a picture of Carl, you could've become Carl." Mrs. Lawrence laughed.

Carl touched his cheek. "I always wanted a twin. That woulda been cool."

I punched Carl's arm. "Ya think? Right now I wanna get rid of this hideous mask." I turned to Mrs. Lawrence. "Can you help me?"

Mrs. Lawrence looked from my face to the drawing again. "Yes, I can help you. Go sit in that chair while I stir this mixture." She walked to the back of the vat, taking the paddle and the picture with her.

I looked around. The only chair I saw was inside a huge purple box-like contraption with golden moons and silver stars splattered all over it. The boxy room looked like it could hold four people if they weren't too large. Carl dragged me over to it. I peered through the door in the front and saw a panel of blinking lights casting an eerie greenish glow over everything inside. Carl stood there with a huge grin on his face while I inspected it. Almost as if he was proud of it, whatever it was.

"What'd ya think, Sam? Do you like my EATT machine? Of course, I don't know if it'll work. I can't find anyone willin' to try it out for me." Carl fiddled with a button on the door.

"Eat machine? Trust you to think about food. What is an eat machine?" I ran my fingers across the seat of the chair.

Carl finished his adjustment on the button and turned to me. "That's E-A-T-T machine, Sam. It means Element Alignment Time Transport. Kenny helped me build it."

"Sounds complicated. When did you build it? Why is it in Mrs. Lawrence's basement?" I couldn't take my eyes off the flashing lights.

"Mrs. Lawrence lets Kenny and me use her basement for our experiments. She says she enjoys the company. She's really cool when you get to know 'er. C'mon, Sam. Sit in the chair and hold on tight."

I sat down and clutched the chair arms so hard I thought I would break a nail. Carl backed off to the middle of the room where a ping-pong table took up a good portion of the floor. A ball and two cushioned paddles were lying on the table, begging someone to pick them up and play a game. I looked down at my swollen, twisted hands, clutching the chair arm, thinking I might never play again if I didn't find some way to get rid of this deformity.

Mrs. Lawrence was back at the vat, stirring the contents with the paddle. From this angle, I saw two steps that led to a platform where she was standing. She wasn't really in the mist that rose from the vat.

"Are you ready, Sam?" she called across the room.

I gulped. "Yes, m'am."

Ready for what? I was sitting in the EATT machine when Carl had already told me no one had tested it. Now I was going to be a guinea pig!

Carl reached under the table and the overhead lights went out. The remaining illumination came from the flashing panel in front of me. Before my eyes could adjust to the gloom, the earsplitting scream filled the air once again and I dug my fingernails into the padded arm of the chair, squinching my eyes tightly shut. It sounded like someone had stepped on a cat's tail. I inhaled sharply and felt my breath catch in my throat.

"Carl?" I opened my eyes and tried to locate Carl. "Are you still here? What's going on?"

There was no answer.

The flashing lights on the panel suddenly went dark as the echoing scream faded away. In the silence that followed, I could hear heavy breathing. My whole body seemed to tingle unpleasantly like when my foot wakes up after I have sat on it too long. My heart pounded against my rib cage, and goose bumps prickled on my arms and legs as the harsh, ragged breathing moved closer and closer. I felt like the room was closing in on me, and I wanted to get out, but I couldn't move. Why couldn't Carl have given me a flashlight? The blanket of darkness surrounded me.

A heavy weight pinned my quaking legs to the chair. Something cold and wet brushed against my cheek and felt slimy against my skin. I hate wet, slimy things, and felt like I wanted to puke. Hot, moist air covered my face. I wanted to scream for Carl to help me, but my tongue felt swollen and stuck to the roof of my mouth. I couldn't make a sound. Why did I let Carl use me as a guinea pig for his invention? What hideous creature had me trapped?

Just as I knew my heart would stop, the ceiling lights flashed on, and I found myself staring into two enormous brown eyes the size of ping-pong balls.

6
Some Snack!

"Tippy, get off Sam," Mrs. Lawrence's voice called out, moving closer to me.

"Tippy?" I managed to gasp, clutching the arms of the black chair tightly. "Who's Tippy?"

"This is Tippy," said Mrs. Lawrence as she pulled a giant black lab off my lap. I relaxed a little but did not release my grip on the arms of the chair as the flickering light from the fire under the vat made the shadows dance all around me. Where had Tippy come from? I didn't remember seeing a dog in the basement before I sat down.

Tippy sat obediently at Mrs. Lawrence's feet, thumping the floor with his tail. Mrs. Lawrence rested her right hand on the dog's black head. Both were looking at me intently as if they expected something from me.

"Wow!" exclaimed Carl. "Sam, you should see yourself. You won't believe it!"

"What now?" I queried. I thought that surely nothing could be worse than electric blue skin, yellow warts, and cypress root hands. Or could it? I might as well find out, so I took a deep breath and closed my eyes, bracing myself for the worst.

"Relax, Sam. It's not that bad," Mrs. Lawrence added. She removed a scarf from her pocket and handed it to Carl. "Carl, would you please tie this scarf over Sam's eyes so she can't peek? Then turn on the overhead light. This will be a pleasant surprise, I think," she chuckled as she waited for Carl to follow her instructions.

Someone, I think it was Mrs. Lawrence, grasped one of my hands.

"We're going to take a walk across the room," her low musical voice sounded near my left ear. "Stand up, Sam." She stayed by my side as we took a few steps. "There is a doorway in front of us. Take a small step down to leave the box."

Hesitantly, I placed my right foot forward and felt gingerly for the step she had mentioned. Once we left the box, her hand remained on mine and we moved slowly. I put out my free hand to feel my way along.

"Don't worry, Sam. There's nothin' in front of you." Carl's familiar voice came from several feet away. I could hear Tippy's toenails clicking on the cement floor of the basement behind me.

At the same time Mrs. Lawrence released my hand, Carl removed the scarf. I blinked rapidly several times to adjust my eyes to the bright light and looked around me. In a mirror over a sink that Mrs. Lawrence had led me to, I caught a glimpse of myself. I couldn't believe my eyes, so I blinked, shook my head, and peered again.

Gazing back at me from the mirror was the most beautiful girl I had ever seen. This couldn't be me. There was no electric blue skin, no yellow warts, and no cypress roots. My lightly tanned skin was the smoothest it had ever been. And my waist-length lifeless reddish brown hair was no longer purple, but was the loveliest shade of auburn I could imagine. I pulled a strand of it over my shoulder and twisted it in my fingers. It was soft and silky, with just the right amount of curl. Without a perm! I smiled. Even the deep dimple to the left of my mouth was beautiful. I had always hated that dimple that everyone else told me was cute. Now, I smiled at my reflection again and the dimple deepened.

"Wow! Thanks! How did you do that? Where did that hideous face and purple hair go?" I glanced at my forearms where Gumby had scratched me earlier. The scratches had vanished along with the hideous face.

"See?" asked Carl. "I knew Mrs. Lawrence could help you."

Mrs. Lawrence, her shoulder-length black hair pulled back in a ponytail, wore a faded pair of jeans and an oversized sweatshirt, and appeared years younger than she usually did at school. In fact, she didn't look much like the science teacher I had last seen at one o'clock when she had dismissed class.

"It was nothing," said Mrs. Lawrence. "The hideous face and the rest of the package are back where they belong." She held up the drawing I had done in first grade. Grinning, she said, "You should be careful what you draw, Sam. You never know when your work might come back to haunt you. Any suggestions about what we should do with this?"

"Burn it!" Carl and I exclaimed simultaneously.

Mrs. Lawrence laughed as she placed the drawing in the flame under the bubbling vat. We watched as the paper started curling and turning brown on the edges. Soon there was nothing left of the old drawing except ashes.

"If only the others had been this easy," Mrs. Lawrence sighed as we turned away from the vat.

"Others? What others? What're you talkin' about?" I turned to Carl. "What others, Carl?" I questioned as Tippy pressed his cold, wet nose into the palm of my hand.

"I'm hungry. Let's go upstairs and get somethin' to eat. You gotta be starved after what you've been through," Carl answered, changing the subject. "I know I'm famished, and all I did was…"

"What did you do, Carl? After what I've been through tonight, this had better be good!"

"Wait!" Mrs. Lawrence interrupted. "Carl's right. You must be hungry. Let's go to the kitchen and get a snack. Then Carl can answer your questions. Don't forget your jackets. Come on." After we retrieved our jackets from the table, she led the way out of the basement room, turning off the lights. Carl and I followed her up the steep flight of stairs into a small hallway. She opened a door on the left and we stepped into the cleanest room I had ever seen. This couldn't be a kitchen. There was nothing in it except a round oak dining table and four chairs.

"Have a seat, Sam. Carl will help me get our snack together, and then we'll tell you everything you want to know," Mrs. Lawrence stated.

She indicated one of the chairs at the table and I sat down, looking around in disbelief at the practically empty room. I couldn't imagine where the snack would come from. The walls were bare. I couldn't see a refrigerator, a stove, or any countertops. Where was the kitchen sink?

Mrs. Lawrence laughed; something she seldom did in class, and snapped her fingers. My jaw dropped and my eyes widened in amazement. Suddenly the kitchen LOOKED like a real kitchen. A built-in stove with a microwave over it now occupied part of one yellow wall. A refrigerator with an ice dispenser stood next to the stove. Cabinets appeared out of nowhere along two walls. The kitchen's sink and built-in dishwasher popped into existence under a window in the rear wall. What was happening? And how did Carl fit into all this?

"How did you do that?" I demanded, as ice clattered in the icemaker.

"Do what?" Mrs. Lawrence replied, as if nothing weird had just occurred. I turned in my chair, pointing at the appliances and cabinets that had just appeared. "Oh that. I snapped my fingers, like this." She snapped her fingers again, and I stared speechlessly as the appliances and cabinets vanished.

Carl grinned from ear to ear. "Isn't that neat? Look, I can do it, too." Carl snapped his fingers. The cabinets and appliances reappeared. "Wanna try it, Sam?"

Of course, I wanted to try it. I just wasn't sure what to do, so I snapped my fingers as I had seen them do. Nothing happened.

Carl snapped his fingers again, and the cabinets and appliances once again vanished.

"That's enough, Carl. Just explain your invention to Sam, after you bring my kitchen back."

Carl grinned at me. "Ready, Sam? Watch carefully."

He snapped his fingers again, and everything returned. This time, I saw the movement of the walls as they withdrew into an almost imperceptible crevice along the floor and ceiling. Now I understood that the appliances and cabinets had not vanished; they were behind the moveable walls that Carl and Mrs. Lawrence somehow controlled by snapping their fingers.

"Kenny and I invented the disappearin' kitchen for Mrs. Lawrence. You activate the walls when you snap your fingers in front of this sensor." He pointed to a small panel beside the light switch.

"Why didn't it work for me?" I asked.

Mrs. Lawrence answered as she crossed the room. "Carl was standing between you and the sensor. That's why nothing happened when you tried it. Carl, come help me."

Mrs. Lawrence opened one of the cabinets and got some plates and cups, which she handed to Carl. Carl set the dishes on the table while Mrs. Lawrence opened another cabinet and took out a cookie jar. Carl removed milk from the refrigerator. The two of them put the snack on the table and then sat down to enjoy it. I only nibbled at my homemade oatmeal cookie, anxious to get to the bottom of the mysterious occurrences.

Finally, after Carl had eaten his cookies, he took a tattered piece of paper out of his pocket. "Do you know what this is?" he asked me.

"No, I don't. What'ya think I am? A mind reader or somethin'?" I responded.

"Exactly!" he almost shouted. He turned to Mrs. Lawrence and continued, "See! I told you she would be perfect, didn't I?"

"What are you babblin' about? Carl, you had better tell me." The strain of the past hour made me snappish. I glared at Carl as he picked up his glass of milk.

Mrs. Lawrence looked from Carl to me and said, "I think you'd better tell her about it before she does something to you that you won't like."

"But she doesn't know that she can," he replied complacently as he set his glass down and took one of my cookies and bit into it.

I narrowed my eyes as I glared at Carl. He chewed slowly on the cookie as he looked cockily at me. Suddenly he started to choke on the cookie and turned red in the face. Then right before my unbelieving eyes, he transformed into a tiny blue butterfly with yellow freckle-like spots. He reminded me of how I had looked not so very long ago. Only he was a butterfly.

"Sam, you need to stop glaring at Carl, or he will disappear completely," Mrs. Lawrence told me calmly when she saw what had transpired.

"But, but I just looked at him," I managed to sputter. "I didn't mean to do anythin' to him. What can I do? How do I get Carl back?"

"You really don't know, do you?" Mrs. Lawrence asked. She reached across the table and touched my hand. As soon as she did, a tingling sensation started at my fingertips and shot through my hand and up my arm.

"You felt that, didn't you?" she inquired.

"What was it?" I asked.

"It's the power within you. You've had this power all your life, but now it's time to learn to use it wisely," she replied.

She put out her other hand and the tiny butterfly - I couldn't think of it as Carl - fluttered into it. She placed the butterfly in the chair where Carl had been. Then she turned to me and announced, "Bring Carl back so that we can explain to you what has been happening - not only to you - but to several of your classmates."

"How can I bring him back? I don't know what to do," I groaned. What if I couldn't bring Carl back? How had I made him vanish in the first place?

"Simply touch him on the head," Mrs. Lawrence instructed me.

So I reached out and touched the tiny butterfly on the head, and before I could remove my index finger from his head, there sat Carl in his chair still munching contentedly on the cookie and clutching the tattered piece of paper he had pulled from his pocket moments before.

"Wow!" I exclaimed. "How did that happen? Can we do it again?"

"What do you mean, 'Wow?' I'm only eatin' a cookie," Carl muttered.

Old Photograph

Suddenly I knew that Carl's ragged piece of paper contained a photograph of our town as it had been in 1890. How could I know that? I hadn't seen any writing on the tattered paper.

"Give me that picture, Carl," I demanded as I snatched the paper from his hand. "You've got some explaining to do. Now, what's going on here?"

I studied the photograph for a minute. The faded ink on the paper seemed to waver and change shape. The old picture had altered to show the location of one house on Spring Street. My house. I couldn't take my eyes off the paper. The image of the house became clearer, and I could see the actual structure as it was in

1890, a small white wooden framed building with a tiny front porch.

I kept my eyes on the frayed piece of paper as the small house started to change again. I could see an addition built onto the back. The date at the top of the page read 1902. The handwritten date on the photograph changed as the house altered, but the address at the bottom of the page never varied. Fascinated, I watched as the structure disappeared in 1928 and reappeared in 1930. Now it was five or six times the size of the original building. The porch, with its roof supported by massive columns ten feet high, stretched the entire length of the front and continued around the side. The shifting scene hypnotized me, and I barely heard a voice calling my name.

"Sam, Sam, can you hear me?" Mrs. Lawrence's voice seemed to come from far away. "What do you see, Sam?"

She gently removed the photograph from my hand and everything around me returned to normal.

"What just happened?" I asked.

"Not now. First, tell me what you saw on this old paper." She held the tattered sheet in front of me. I automatically reached for it, but she pulled it back out of my reach. "You mustn't touch it again. At least, not yet. What did you see, Sam?" Mrs. Lawrence rubbed the back of her neck.

I thought for a minute before answering her question, massaging my temples in an effort to concentrate. "I didn't see much. The picture focused on one location that was the address where I live now. I know that because the address at the bottom of the picture never altered. The house at that address kept changing appearance. At one point, it disappeared completely and reappeared as a mansion. It was huge and the porch went all the way around the house. Oh, yeah! The date at the top of the page changed as the buildin' changed. What does all that mean? Why did I see it and you couldn't?" I stopped to catch my breath as Mrs. Lawrence tapped the photograph several times with her index finger. "Mrs. Lawrence, can I ask you something?" I waited for her reply.

"I don't know, can you?" She answered in her teacher voice.

"Sorry. *May* I ask you a question?" I corrected myself, as I had done many times in class. "You remember earlier when Carl was a butterfly?"

"What do you mean, I was a butterfly? When was I a butterfly? I wasn't no butterfly! Girls! You sure do get funny ideas," Carl interrupted, as he stood up to return the milk carton to the refrigerator.

I rolled my eyes in his direction. "You said somethin' about power within me. What kind of power? How do I use it? There's just so much happenin' I don't understand."

Mrs. Lawrence glanced at her watch. "All right, Sam. You should know what's happening since it involves you." She looked at me intently. "You possess the power to see what others can't see. Your gift enables you to see beyond the surface of a picture, which is why you saw the houses at your address changing through the years. You may not understand everything you see, but you'll learn." She smiled sadly, a smile that never reached her eyes. "Right now, we have something important to do."

She turned to Carl who stood near the table feeling his shoulders. He was muttering something under his breath about butterflies and wings.

"Come on, Carl. Get Tippy and let's get to Sam's house before it's too late. Sam, trust us. We'll explain everything as soon as we can." Mrs. Lawrence stood, gathered the dishes we'd used and carried them to the sink.

"Let's go!" called Mrs. Lawrence as she handed me my jacket and pulled me toward the door. Carl rushed to catch up, while Tippy barked excitedly.

We dashed out the back door into the garage as Tippy ran ahead and then came back to us as if to say move faster.

Mrs. Lawrence used a remote to open the garage door as we piled into her van for the two-mile ride to my home. Three blocks from my house, the van's engine sputtered, coughed, and died. Leaving the vehicle at the curb, we sprinted the remaining distance.

It didn't take long for Mrs. Lawrence to leave us behind. She moved faster than a cheetah after a gazelle. She was already half a block ahead of us when Carl scooped me up and continued running. Tippy raced ahead to keep pace with the teacher.

As abruptly as our run had begun, it ended. Mrs. Lawrence was waiting for us in front of my house. Carl set me on my feet, breathing hard through his mouth. I glanced around and noted that Uncle Art's convertible no longer sat in the driveway.

Carl turned to Mrs. Lawrence and asked, "D'ya think we made it in time?"

"The only way to find out is to go inside," she replied, not even winded from the exertion of running three blocks. What was she, superhuman or something? If Carl was breathing hard after our journey, Mrs. Lawrence should have been too.

"Gimme your key, Sam," he panted, extending his hand toward me.

"I can't find it," I answered patting my pockets. "I guess I left in such a hurry that I forgot to take the key with me. What're we goin' to do now?"

Mrs. Lawrence observed, "If you left in a hurry, maybe you forgot to lock the door, too."

Carl bounded up the steps to the porch and turned the knob. It did not budge. "Wait here." He began moving along the porch toward the side of the house. "I know how to get in."

Mrs. Lawrence and I stood on the porch waiting for Carl to reappear. A minute later, he returned carrying the front door key in his right hand. "I found it under the flower pot by the side door." He puffed his chest out as if he had done something unusual. In all the excitement, I had forgotten about that hidden key, but I didn't want Carl to know.

"Good. You saved me havin' to go get it. Now, could you stop floppin' around like a chicken with its head cut off and unlock this door?"

Carl inserted the key into the lock, twisted it to the right, and shoved the door inward. He led the way through the door, peering cautiously into the gloomy interior. Mrs. Lawrence flipped the light switch to the living room. I heard a popping sound as a bright flash almost blinded me. The bulb had blown.

We started up the darkened stairs with Mrs. Lawrence in the lead. I was next, followed closely by Carl. I could hear Tippy's toenails clicking on the steps ahead of us.

At the top of the stairs, Mrs. Lawrence turned to me. "Which room is yours?"

"That one." I pointed to the room at the end of the hall to the left, and she started in that direction with her little parade following her.

As we entered the darkened bedroom, I could just make out a figure moving near the dresser. I wanted to turn and run, but with Carl behind me, I had no choice, so I went on. Mrs. Lawrence paused at the edge of the dresser as the figure approached her. "It's okay, Tippy." She snapped her fingers and the dog sat near her feet, with his tongue lolling out of the side of his mouth. "We'll take care of it now."

"Take care of what?" My stomach felt hollow like I hadn't eaten in several days.

She glanced behind the dresser, pulled it out from the wall about fifteen inches, and apparently satisfied with what she saw, turned to Carl and me, smiling. "It looks like we made it with time to spare," she announced. She walked over to my window and adjusted the curtains so that a small amount of streetlight could enter.

I wondered what she was looking for and tried to see around her to see what was behind the dresser to make her smile. All I could see was the small closed door with its dented brass knob.

"Come on," she told Carl and me. "Let's sit on the bed and talk for a few minutes." Carl sat at the head of the bed leaning back against my pillows. I sat at the foot with Mrs. Lawrence between Carl and me. She turned to me and began, "Sam, Carl and I owe you an explanation and now is as good a time as any."

"Wait!" Carl exclaimed. "Don't we need to . . ." He stopped in mid-sentence as a hideous screeching sound filled the bedroom.

I clapped my hands over my ears to muffle the sound.

8
Samuel

"Listen carefully, Sam." Mrs. Lawrence glanced toward the dresser. "In a few minutes, you will find yourself facing a truth you never could have imagined. You need to go in there and convince the gingerbread man to come with you to my house. Once we have him there, we can straighten everything out."

"I'll turn blue again," I whimpered. "I don't want to go in there again!"

Carl touched my hand gently, offering words of encouragement. "It'll be okay, Sam. I'm sorry I put you in this position. If only I hadn't spilled that mixture from the vat on the photograph, we wouldn't be here now." He smiled at me glumly with his eyes lowered, and I found myself smiling back. I couldn't stay mad at him.

"Relax, Carl. You didn't make me do anythin'. Stop blamin' yourself for something you didn't do." I squeezed his hand to reassure him that he had done nothing wrong. If I found out later that he had caused these strange events, then I could choke him.

"I don't know if I can do this. I don't think I'm the person you need to help you," I turned to Mrs. Lawrence.

"You'll do just fine. Just convince the gingerbread man to come back with you. He knows more than I do about your special 'gift'."

"What special 'gift'? Does this have anything to do with that power you mentioned earlier? What are you talking about?"

"The answers to your questions will come soon." Mrs. Lawrence stood. "We must be ready."

Tippy began to bark urgently. There was a scraping sound from behind the dresser, and the brass knob started to turn slowly, catching a glint of light from the distant street lamp.

Mrs. Lawrence pushed Carl and me toward the dresser.

"Carl, go with Sam and help her bring the gingerbread man back. Go on, you two. I can't help you now. This town needs you."

"Why does the town need us?" I asked as the doorknob continued turning.

"A group of rebels is planning to take over the town. People won't be safe because the rebels will be in control. We can't let that happen, can we, Sam?" In the dim light, I saw the slight throbbing of pulse at her temple increase as she mentioned the rebellious group who wanted to control our small town.

Tippy barked again and began to growl as suddenly the same beam of greenish light that had lit my room earlier this evening appeared. How long ago had that been? It seemed like forever. Was the gingerbread man waiting on the other side of that door? If not, how would Carl and I locate him? A tiny voice, which seemed to come from the light beam, exclaimed, "There you are! I've been waiting for you. Where were you?"

A rustling of clothing behind me caught my attention. Mrs. Lawrence must have moved closer to the dresser. "Oh, hi, Mrs. Lawrence. I didn't see you back there," the tiny voice called out. "Are you coming with us? No, how silly of me. Of course, you can't come with us."

Why couldn't Mrs. Lawrence enter the small door? Then I remembered the rhyme the voice had used the last time. Something about a mortal not being able to use the door. Was that why the science teacher couldn't get the gingerbread man herself? Why could I enter the door? Wasn't I mortal? Was Carl not a mortal either? What was happening here?

The door opened as far as it could before it bumped against the dresser, and Carl and I ducked to step through into the eerily lit world on the other side. The green-sprinkled grass sparkled in the light from the beam. The rest of the candy garden, at least what I could see of it, looked the same as it had earlier, except that the dime-size buds had started to open. The only thing moving besides Carl and me was the beam of light, which hovered near the foot of a staircase that I hadn't seen on my earlier visit. It looked like the one in my house.

The licorice treetops were motionless. Where was the gingerbread man?

"Where is the gingerbread man?" I took a step toward the light.

The light drifted closer to the stairs. "He's waiting for you."

"Then he knows I'm here?" If he knew, why wasn't he here to meet me?

"He knows everything. Is there anything else you would like to ask me before we go?" The voice paused.

I took a deep breath. "How do you know Mrs. Lawrence? Why couldn't she come through that door? Why didn't you tell me the whole truth the last time I was here?"

"Truth? What truth? Is there any truth? Wouldn't you rather have reality? What's true for one may not be true for all, but reality is." The voice paused as the light pulsed brighter.

"I want to know how you know so much about my family," I stamped my foot like a child about to throw a tantrum.

"Impatient, Sam?" the voice taunted me. "You'll have to wait for your answers, Miss Inquisitive." I felt Carl's breath against my neck as he followed me into the candy garden. "Oh, hi, Carl. I didn't know you would be coming with us. Well, let's get started since Sam is soooo impatient."

"Hi, Tiny. Has anything happened that we should know about before we begin our quest?" Carl replied.

"Anything? Nothing. Something? Everything. You should know better than to ask that question, Carl." The voice started to fade away and the light grew dimmer.

"C'mon, Sam. We need to follow Tiny while we can. If she fades away completely, it'll be too late for us to accomplish what we came for. We gotta find your gingerbread man."

Carl gently pushed me toward the beam of light. As I entered the beam, it became brighter again. Carl entered the beam with me, and we immediately floated into the air and sped toward the head of the stairs. The light deposited us at the top of the steps and faded into the background.

"Hello, Samantha. We meet again." The voice belonged to the gingerbread man, but the speaker was a middle-aged man who looked remarkably like my Uncle Art. "Are you ready to learn the truth, inquisitive one?"

"Uncle Art?"

"No, Samantha."

I glanced at Carl who was grinning like he had just made an unassisted triple play. He winked at me and backed off a step.

I turned to the man with Uncle Art's face and voice.

"Why do you sound and look like my Uncle Art? Where is the gingerbread man? Who *are* you?"

"I am your great-great grandfather, Samuel."

"My great-great grandfather? No way! You don't look old enough to be a great-great grandfather." I stepped back to get a better look at him. His full head of dark brown hair gleamed in the twilight. He was at least six inches taller than Carl, which meant he had to be at least six feet four inches tall. He didn't look like he could be more than forty, which would make him about the same age as Uncle Art.

"You can call me Sam." Samuel smiled and little wrinkles formed around his eyes.

"Won't that be confusin'?" I asked.

"Why?"

"Well, everyone calls me Sam."

"Oh, that's right. How could I have forgotten? Then you can call me Samuel. Now, Samantha, are you ready to learn the truth?"

"I guess so," I answered frowning. I really wasn't sure that I was ready for the truth. After all, it appeared that I had a great-great grandfather the same age as Dad and Uncle Art and he lived behind my dresser in a world made out of candy. Obviously, that couldn't be true. Could I trust whatever he told me to be the truth?

"Then let's get started. Carl, it's good to see you again. Are you taking good care of my Samantha?"

"Yes, Sir," Carl nodded his head and Samuel smiled.

The beam of light, which had hovered nearby, finally began to move again. Samuel took one hand as Carl took the other, and we stepped into the unusual light source.

The Beginning

When the light reached its destination, the three of us stood in a large meadow near a gigantic weeping willow. Under the tree, a young couple sat on a blanket, talking quietly and sharing a picnic meal from a wicker basket. She wore a simple loose-fitting lavender dress. The young man, dressed casually in a loose white shirt and black pants, couldn't have been much older than twenty. A black lab puppy chewed quietly on a bone that the young man tossed to him.

We sat on the grass and silently watched the couple for a few minutes, unable to hear the conversation between them. Finally, Samuel spoke in a near whisper, "Those are my parents as they were in 1890, just six months before I was born. And this is where the story begins, Samantha."

Carl had wandered a few feet away and was examining one of the candy plants with the blue and green buds.

Samuel leaned toward me, his eyes glistening with unshed tears.

"I was the oldest of three boys. When my mother died, I was seventeen. On her deathbed, she said she had to tell us a family secret." Samuel paused and swiped his hand over his eyes. "She confessed that she was a descendent of one of the Salem witches who had escaped death when the trials ended. She revealed that as long as the children of her descendents were males, the magic powers would be dormant. There were no females born into the family until…"

"Until I was born?" I supplied, taking a deep breath.

"Yes."

I leaned toward him. "Tell me more about your parents. Did your father know your mother was a witch? Why couldn't she use magic to cure herself and live longer?"

"Still curious, I see," Samuel chuckled as he watched the lab run toward a brook in the distance. "As I was growing up, I had no idea that my mother was a witch. I never saw her use her powers in any way, not even when our house burned one Christmas Eve. She didn't even use her powers when it rained for an entire week, and the fields all flooded, destroying the crops." He clasped his hands behind his head and lay back on the grass. "She could have used her powers to keep from dying, but she chose not to." He sighed. "Gradually, I realized she had moved on to a better life. When Father died, he joined her in her new life, and the last time I spoke to them, they were very happy."

"You spoke to them? I thought you said they died?"

"The body may die, Sam, but the spirit does not."

"But how could you speak to them? Wouldn't you need magic powers to do that?" I sat on the grass gazing at the couple under the tree. "Do you have magic powers, Samuel?"

Samuel ran his fingers through his thick dark hair. "Yes, Sam, but my powers are limited. I have latent magical power, but a very good friend of mine bestowed limited active powers upon me. I can see into the future."

We sat side by side, neither of us speaking for a while. Carl had picked one of the blue buds that had begun to open. At last, Samuel turned to look at me. He lifted a strand of my auburn hair and rubbed it between his fingers.

"Do you understand what I have told you? Do you understand that you are special?" He released my hair, placed his hand under my chin, and lifted my face until our eyes met. "Samantha, you were born with magic powers. The truth is," he paused, "you are a witch."

What kind of nonsense was this? Me, a witch? I don't think so.

The words popped out of my mouth before I could stop them. "Are you sure? Don't witches cast magic spells and change people into animals and stuff like that?"

"Witches can do almost anything they want to do," Samuel smiled at me. "Remember what you did to Carl at Mrs. Lawrence's?"

"Yeah, but I don't know how I did it. It just happened," I grinned at the memory of Carl as a tiny butterfly. How did Samuel know about that?

Samuel lowered his head to mine and whispered, "You realize he doesn't remember what happened?"

"Yes, I picked up on that earlier when he denied ever being a butterfly," I whispered back.

"What about Carl?" I asked suddenly as it occurred to me that he had passed through the small door. "Is Carl a witch or a warlock or whatever you call a guy witch?"

"You'll have to ask him about that," he chuckled as Carl started back toward us carrying the opened bud gingerly in his palm. When he reached us, he reached down and pulled me to my feet. He placed the budding blue candy flower in my left hand and closed my fingers over it. When he released my hand, I opened it so that I could see the candy flower. It was almost completely unfolded. What had the gingerbread man said this blue flower was? Intelligence? No, that was the bed of lemon drops. Curiosity? I think that was the orange wedges. Think, Sam. What did he say? I know! The blue and green dime-sized buds were the understanding plant. The gingerbread man said they would open soon. Was he talking about *my* understanding? Of course, he was. After all, it was *my* garden. I deposited the candy in my pocket.

Samuel stood up and brushed the grass from his pants. "Is there anything else you want to ask?"

"Why didn't Mrs. Lawrence just tell me that I'm a witch?" My voice rose, filled with indignation.

"You wouldn't have believed her, would you?" Samuel asked.

"Probably not," I admitted as I twirled a long strand of hair idly through my fingers. "But can you blame me? After all, everyone knows that witches don't exist."

"Don't they? How would you explain what has happened to you today? If it isn't witchcraft, what is it? A dream?"

"But the gingerbread man had your voice!" I wasn't quite ready to believe him.

"Ah, yes. The gingerbread man. I didn't want to scare you, and if you can't trust a gingerbread man, who can you trust, eh, Sam?"

"How can you explain the light beam? And the voice I heard?" I needed some answers. Was Samuel the gingerbread man? Did he know why we were here?

"They are real," replied Samuel. "The light and the voice are the guardians of the portals between the past and the present. That's why they were near the door."

"So that's what Tiny meant when she said she was a keeper of the portal which couldn't be used by a mortal. And that explains how I could use the door."

Suddenly Carl spoke up. It was the first time he had spoken since we arrived at the weeping willow tree. "Uh, I hate to break up this little interrogation, but we really need to get the gingerbread man and get back to Mrs. Lawrence. It's already eleven."

"You're right, Carl. Let's go see your Mrs. Lawrence." Samuel turned toward the tree as he spoke. His parents had left, but Tiny was there, waiting for us. Once again, we entered the light beam. This time, our journey terminated beside the little door that led from this dimension into my bedroom.

"I'll be right back." Carl gave me a thumbs up and headed toward the fudge patch.

"Samuel, how do Carl and Mrs. Lawrence know about you?" I looked up at him.

Samuel rubbed the fingers of his right hand back and forth along his left jaw and leaned down to look me in the eye. "Can you keep a secret?"

I grinned at him, remembering that we had had this conversation the first time we met. "Sure."

He cupped his hand close to my ear and whispered, "They, too, possess magical powers."

My mouth dropped open. Carl and Mrs. Lawrence had magical powers? That could explain many weird things that had happened. Why hadn't they told me? For that matter, why hadn't I figured it out for myself?

Samuel placed his index finger across his lips in a hushing motion. "This is our secret, Sam. They'll tell you when they're ready."

Carl returned from his little side trip clutching fudge squares in one hand. His eyes twinkled as he handed two squares to me. I bit into one of the pieces of fudge and rolled it around in my mouth enjoying the treat that tasted like apple pie. I offered one of the pieces to Samuel, but he smiled and shook his head.

"Let's find Mrs. Lawrence." My great-great grandfather chuckled. "Didn't she tell you to bring back the gingerbread man? Let's humor her, shall we? Sam, hand me the purple candy blossom that I placed behind your ear." I reached into the pocket of my jeans and withdrew the candy he wanted. He placed the blossom behind his own ear. As he did, a tremendous flash of light surrounded him. Carl and I jumped, dropping the remaining fudge as we covered our eyes to protect them from the glare.

"It's okay to look now." The voice belonged to Samuel, but the three-foot tall gingerbread man stood where Samuel had been only the moment before.

Just then, the door flew open, and Tippy greeted us with a joyous bark. I looked around the bedroom, lit only by my desk lamp, but found no trace of Mrs. Lawrence. The three of us stepped through the door just as another screech broke the silence. I screamed, too, clutching Carl's left arm and feeling his biceps tense as I dug my fingernails into him.

10
Getting Stronger

The scream faded away, leaving us in silence.

Carl's face twisted in pain, and he began prying my fingers off his arm one at a time. "Hey, let up a bit, Sam. You're gonna hav'ta cut your nails if you're gonna dig 'em into me like that. I didn't know you were so strong."

"Sorry," I mumbled as I tried to relax. "It's just that those screams are starting to get on my nerves."

"Yeah, I know what you mean. They're getting on mine, too," Carl agreed as his rubbed his upper arm where my fingers had left their mark.

"That should be the last of them. Four people in this town won't be in control of their own bodies much longer," the gingerbread man said under his breath as he scratched Tippy behind the ears. Tippy's rear end wagged back and forth.

"You like that, eh, boy?" Samuel asked the lab who was now trying to lick Samuel's face. "Whoa! Down, boy. I know you're glad to see me, but until I'm Samuel again, I can't have you licking my face off, literally," he laughed.

"Where is Mrs. Lawrence? I thought she'd be here when we got back." I glanced in the mirror, relieved to see that I had not changed into the blue creature from my previous visit.

"I did, too," the gingerbread man agreed, shutting the small door behind us. He helped Carl put the dresser back in place. Tippy began prancing around me and almost knocked me down when he jumped up to put his paws on my shoulders. He settled back on all four feet, grabbed the hem of my sweatshirt, and kept pulling until he had dragged me to my desk in the corner of the room. Mrs. Lawrence had left a note propped against my science book.

Dear Sam and Carl,

I couldn't wait any longer, but I know you'll join me as soon as you can. Take care of the gingerbread man. See you soon.

Mrs. Lawrence

"Look." I handed the note to the gingerbread man. Carl read it over his shoulder.

"We'd better go. If we don't get to Mrs. Lawrence's soon, it's goin' to be too late," Carl muttered. "They're probably there now waitin' for us."

The gingerbread man pulled himself up to his full height. "All right, young man, lead the way to Mrs. Lawrence's house."

"Wait a minute," I put my hand on Carl's arm. "Samuel can't go out in the street like that," I pointed at the gingerbread man. "How can we get him there safely?"

"Sam's right, Carl. We can't let people see a gingerbread man walking down the street. What are we going to do?"

Carl looked at the gingerbread man and then looked at me. He rubbed his chin the way he always did when he was getting an idea. Suddenly he snapped his fingers.

"I know what to do. Sam, get one of your coats, and we'll put it on Samuel. We can let him wear one with a hood so he can keep his face hidden, kinda like you did when you were blue."

Samuel, the gingerbread man, nodded in agreement, as his chocolate frosted eyes lifted at the corners. "That could work. It's worth a try, anyway. Sam, do you have an extra coat with a hood?"

"Sure. I'll get it."

Once the gingerbread man had wrapped himself in my coat, he could have passed for a short kid as long as no one saw him up close or got a whiff of his spicy Christmassy scent.

With Carl leading the way and Tippy bringing up the rear, we crept quietly down the stairs. We tiptoed past the living room, where the flickering glow from the TV revealed Art and Kate sitting on the sofa with their backs to the door. We left the security of the house behind and walked quickly down the dimly lit streets, ducking into shadows whenever a vehicle approached. Mrs. Lawrence's van no longer sat abandoned where we had left it. She must've gotten it started. The feeling of someone following us returned as we passed the library.

I touched Carl on the shoulder, but before I could say anything he whispered, "I know, Sam. I feel it too."

When we reached Mrs. Lawrence's, Carl and I were both breathing heavily, and my sides had started to ache. Carl held out his right hand in a signal to Samuel and me, cautioning us to be quiet. We tiptoed onto the front porch where Carl, who was in the lead, halted abruptly. I bumped into him as he whirled around to face Samuel and me.

"What's wrong now?" I whispered.

He whispered back, "You'll have to open the door, Sam. They're getting stronger, and I'm afraid I don't have the power to overcome them."

My eyes widened. "What are you talking about? You're stronger and bigger than me. Why should I go first?"

"Not that kinda strong, Sam. The magic kinda strong. No time to explain now. Just open the door so we can get to the basement before midnight." Carl pushed me toward the door.

I crossed my arms, stuck my chin out, and my tilted my head back a little. "Not until you tell me who 'they' are," I answered stubbornly.

Carl sighed loudly, "Sam, do you know what a familiar is?"

"Sure. Everybody knows that a witch has a familiar, sometimes a cat or a dog, who helps with magic spells."

"Close enough," Samuel said. "Carl senses that there are familiars on the other side of that door. They have rebelled against their masters and have joined forces to take over this town. These particular familiars are bullies who like doing things their way. Once they have control of the town and its citizens, they plan to expand and take control of the state, then the nation, and then the world. They escaped into this dimension when you first opened the door in your bedroom."

"Why are they here, at Mrs. Lawrence's?"

"Apparently, they followed you and Carl earlier in the evening. Since you're the one they react to, you had better do as Carl says and open the door," Samuel agreed.

"Yeah," Carl squeezed my hand. "And it looks like you're the one who has to stop 'em."

Was he crazy? Me keep some rebelling familiars from taking over the town? Like that was gonna happen. Sure, Sam. You can do it. You're a witch. You can do anything. Wanna bet?

"Right, I'm going to stop 'em," was my hesitant reply. "What do I need to do? How am I going to stop 'em?

What am I supposed to do, just twitch my nose, mutter a magic spell and turn 'em into toads? C'mon Carl, get real!"

Carl's hands moved toward my throat like he wanted to throttle me. The gingerbread man reached up, touched Carl's elbow, and then turned to me. "You have to get us through that door and into the basement without touching any of the familiars. So far, there are only four of them. That much I know because we have heard that earsplitting scream four times. Each time we hear a scream, another one of the familiars takes possession of one of your classmates."

"Are you sure I can do this?" I hesitated.

"Samantha, listen to me. You can do anything you put your mind to. The only one who can stop you is you." Samuel threw back the hood of his jacket.

Carl jabbed his thumb in Samuel's direction. "Yeah. What he said,"

Samuel stood on tiptoe and patted me reassuringly on the shoulder. "We've got to move now. Time is running out. We're depending on you, Samantha,"

They have more confidence in me than I do. I just hope I don't disappoint them.

11
Midnight

Carl took my left hand as I tentatively reached for the doorknob with my right hand. My pulse throbbed in my fingertips as I turned the knob slowly and pushed the front door open a few inches. I entered the house slowly and paused just inside the doorway. There was no sound inside the living room and the only light came from the face of a digital clock on the mantle. The time was eleven forty-five. We had fifteen minutes to get to the basement.

We had taken five or six steps into the room when a soft scratching noise from the study caught our attention. The heavy study door crashed open. We froze in our tracks. At first, I couldn't see anything, but as my eyes adjusted to the dimness of the house, I made out a shape moving stealthily toward us from the room across the hall.

The gingerbread man stretched out his doughy hand to touch my right hand and I knew what I had to do.

"Stop!" I commanded in a voice I hoped wasn't as shaky as I felt. "If you take another step, you'll be sorry!" My knees were knocking together and I wished I had gone to the bathroom earlier.

Complete silence met my announcement. The shadowy figure paused about five feet away from where I stood with the gingerbread man and Carl, just inside the front door. The silence grew until finally I heard a giggle from the vicinity of the motionless shadow.

"Now, Sam. Is that any way to talk to a friend?" I knew that voice. It belonged to Dalton, my lab partner in science class. "What'ya gonna do to make me sorry? D'ya think I'm afraid of a girl? Besides, if ya look around, you'll see that we outnumber you slightly. Right, guys?"

"Band kids need a life." The deep voice filled the room.

"You know it!" A shadow rose from behind the couch.

"Who, me?" The curtains shifted as another figure stepped into the room.

Three distinct voices from three different directions. And I knew every one of them. Now it was my turn to giggle. Dalton couldn't find his way out of a paper bag with the lights on, as Uncle Art would say. He acted tough, swaggering around as if he owned the world when his friends were around, but when he was alone he couldn't decide if his hair was light brown or dark blonde. Dalton didn't scare me.

"Band kids need a life," the words rang through the room again. That voice belonged to Barrett, probably the most dangerous of the four. Barrett liked to throw his considerable weight around and always picked on the kids in the band. I had seen him stand in the hall before homeroom yelling insults at the younger band students as they took their instruments to the music room. He was the same height as Carl, but he weighed at least fifty pounds more. Usually, he was the one leading the others into trouble. Why was he allowing Dalton to do the talking?

The third voice belonged to Darren. He could be a nice guy when he wasn't around the other three, but most of the time he was trying to impress his friends and let them know how tough he could be. "You know it," he repeated. His dark skin blended into the darkness around him, and his white teeth gleamed in the faint light.

"Who, me?" That could only be Damien. He and Darren liked to pick on the smaller students, but they liked to work together. Damien's ebony skin also faded into the darkness so now I was looking at two faceless grins, floating in the darkness. On any other day, the sight would have turned my knees to water, but today I had to clamp my hands over my mouth to stifle my laugh.

My giggle escaped and immediately Darren demanded, "What are you laughin' at?"

"Who, me? I ain't laughin' at nothin'."

"I wasn't talkin' to you," Darren called across the living room to Damien.

"You talkin' to me?" Damien baited his friend.

"Shut up! Both of you," Barrett roared. "We got better things to do than liss'n to your comedy routine. Get over here."

"What'cha doin' givin' the orders?" Dalton whined. "I'm the leader this time. You said so. You promised."

"You wanna be in charge, you make 'em shut up," Barrett said with a sneer.

I could feel the muscles in my neck start to relax. Now that I knew whom the familiars had chosen to act as go-betweens, I thought this should be a piece of cake. It might even be fun to make these four squirm a little. Carl must have agreed because I could feel him shaking with suppressed laughter. Samuel had stepped behind Carl so that the intruders couldn't see him. If they caught sight of a gingerbread man, there was no telling what they'd do.

"Now turn the light on an' let's see what we got here," Dalton had taken over again.

I couldn't let them turn the light on. They'd see the gingerbread man, and then we'd never get them to the basement. I could almost hear their laughter when they saw him. These bullies could hurt Samuel, and I couldn't allow that to happen.

"Stay where you are! If any of you touch that light switch, I won't be responsible for what happens to you," my voice came out as a whisper that sounded more like a hiss to me.

"I already asked ya what ya gonna do," Dalton reminded me.

I felt Carl shifting his position behind me. He and Samuel were depending on me, and I could do nothing but stand there, unable to find my voice again or respond to the taunt in Dalton's tone.

"Speechless, huh?" sneered Dalton. "The four o' us will rule th' world. No one can stop us. Right, guys?"

"Band kids drool." Barrett bowed slightly toward Dalton.

"We're bad. You know it." Darren muttered the words like a mantra.

"Who, me?" Damien repeated.

Carl stepped forward. "Dalton, you seem to be the leader here. Let's go down to the rec room in the basement and discuss this situation," Carl edged his way toward the door to the hallway at the rear of the living room, keeping himself between the threatening familiars and Samuel.

The other three started forward to block our progress. I paused as Dalton reached for my arm. Just as he was about to touch me, a huge black shape flew at him from the shadows and knocked him flat on his back on the floor. Tippy stood over his captive, growling, and wouldn't let him get up. One down, three to go. Only eight minutes left until midnight. We still had to get this group into the basement.

"Call off th' dog, Sam," whined Dalton. "We'll talk this out, and you'll see we're not the enemy."

"We don't trust you," I ignored the pleading in his voice. "You lead the way to the basement, Damien. Once you three are there, we'll let Dalton get up."

Dalton was almost in tears as Tippy lowered his gigantic head and growled again. "Damien, do as Sam says. I can't get up until she calls off this monster," Dalton wailed.

"Who, me?" came the predictable reply.

"Yeah, you!" Dalton was frantic now. Tippy stood straddling Dalton's prone figure.

"Damien!" Dalton screamed as Tippy bared his teeth. Damien finally seemed to get the message and turned reluctantly toward the door. Darren trailed along readily enough, but Barrett wasn't going to be as easy.

"Five minutes," Carl whispered in my ear. Like I needed reminding. Carl winked at me before he and the gingerbread man shadowed the two familiars from the room.

"Well, Barrett, we're waiting on you," I stated.

"You'll keep..." Dalton's screech cut Barrett off when Tippy put his nose right against Dalton's and growled louder and more fiercely than before.

Barrett clapped his hands over his ears as he turned and ran toward the rear hallway door.

"Good boy, Tippy," I praised the lab petting his head. "Let him up."

Promptly, Tippy moved away from the prone familiar, and once Dalton had scrambled to his feet, herded him from the living room.

My knees were shaking as I entered the basement, pulling the door shut behind me just as the voice from the clock on the mantle announced, "Twelve A.M."

12
No Memory

Mrs. Lawrence stood at the foot of the stairs, blocking Darren and Damien who cowered on the third step from the bottom. She had her hands on her hips and her head cocked to one side as she studied the faces of our captives. She glanced up at us, her eyes lingering on the gingerbread man, and remarked, "That was very close, Sam. You're lucky that Dalton's familiar is afraid of dogs. But I guess that's to be expected, since his familiar is really a cat when he's not occupying someone else's body." She actually chortled when the four familiars who occupied the bodies of my four classmates winced at the word 'familiar'. "Oh, yes," she added. "I know exactly who you are, and why you're here."

Carl nudged Darren and Damien as Mrs. Lawrence stepped aside. "Yeah, and we're also lucky that the real Dalton is a follower. That would've been really rough if Barrett had been the one in charge." Carl followed Darren and Damien down the steps as the gingerbread man scooted past them to stand beside Mrs. Lawrence. Carl cleared his throat. "Speaking of followin', which of you four clowns has been following Sam and me this evenin'?"

Darren fidgeted uneasily and wouldn't look at Carl or me. One mystery solved.

"I didn't do nothin' wrong. It's still a free country, ain't it?" Darren's muttered reply was barely audible.

"Not if I have anythin' to say 'bout it, it ain't," Barrett growled.

Tippy growled in return and Barrett backed up a step as Dalton cowered behind him and whimpered, "Keep that beast away from me."

Mrs. Lawrence clapped her hands once, sharply. "That's enough nonsense. Since we're all here, it's time to get something accomplished." Mrs. Lawrence was all business now. She turned to the fearsome foursome and asked in her sternest teacher voice, "What were you going to do to this town and its inhabitants?"

"Nothing," Dalton sulked. "We wasn't gonna do nothing."

Mrs. Lawrence's eyes narrowed slightly, and her lips compressed into a thin line. I had seen that expression before, and so had Dalton. He hastily corrected his statement.

"I'm sorry. I meant to say we weren't going to do noth… anything. I meant anything." Dalton's lower lip quivered.

"Then why are you here?" Mrs. Lawrence pointed at Dalton. "And it had better be the truth. If you lie to me, you will answer to my dear friend and familiar, Tippy." Damien and Darren shuffled their feet as Barrett and Dalton exchanged a glance. None of them spoke. Mrs. Lawrence took a step toward the familiars. "I know that you call yourselves the Bad Deeds Double Duo. I would have expected four enterprising familiars who managed to escape into this dimension to be more creative than to use the initials of these four boys to give yourselves a name. I know about your plans to take over this town. Not a bad idea to choose bullies to do your dirty work, but you should've chosen hosts who wouldn't be intimidated by a dog."

Now it was my turn. "We also know that in your original form you're all cats. You don't really like dogs, especially large ones. I think we'll send you back where you belong in a different form. Yes, I think we should turn you into small yappy dogs. Do you think your owners will like that?" I narrowed my eyes and nodded as I regarded the four. "Yes, I like the idea of changing you into Chihuahuas, but I think I need to make you special. Any ideas how to make them special, Carl?"

Darren and Damien hung their heads while Dalton's eyes widened and he began whimpering. Barrett snorted, tossed his head, and muttered, "You don't scare me."

Carl rubbed his chin and tapped his forefinger on his nose a few times. "Good idea, Sam. Let's make 'em special." He paused. "Let's put little pink bows in their hair and dress them in those little ballerina skirts like those dogs in the circus wear."

"Great idea, Carl. They'll be so cute." I faced our four prisoners again. "The only way you'll ever have any other form is if you come back through that small door again. And Samuel may have something to say about that."

"Not only that," Mrs. Lawrence pointed at the four, "you won't be permitted to practice witchcraft any more. The Witches' Council will see to it that your days as familiars are over."

Samuel gazed at the four young men solemnly with his brown frosting eyes. "We won't turn you into dogs yet. We'll leave you with some dignity, which is more than you planned to do for your hosts. Before you leave the bodies of these four young men, you will erase all memories of this experience from their minds. They will remember nothing. Is that clear?"

The Bad Deeds Double Duo nodded their heads meekly.

"Tippy, escort your prisoners to the EATT machine." Mrs. Lawrence pointed to the purple box.

"This is great! I couldn't find any volunteers for my machine, and now I have four," Carl grinned from ear to ear. "I hope it works. You know I haven't tested it yet." He turned to me. "No offense, Sam, but you don't count." He looked at Mrs. Lawrence. "Do you think it'll handle four at a time?" I saw her wink at him.

"Of course it'll work. You've done a great job on it. Now set the date control timer, and let's get rid of our uninvited guests."

Carl entered the EATT machine to adjust the control knobs. He was making the required adjustments when Barrett made a break for the stairs. The gingerbread man tackled him, knocking his legs out from under him. Then he sat on Barrett's chest and held him down while the other three familiars scattered. Dalton dived under the table, curled up in a ball, and covered his head with his arms. Damien sprinted towards the stairs, but swerved to avoid tripping over Tippy, and ran into the tiny closet under the stairway. Darren ran into the EATT machine and tried to hide under the control panel. Carl grabbed Darren, slammed him into the chair, and strapped him in. Next, he went after Damien, dragged him from the closet, put him in a chokehold like I'd seen on television, and marched him to the machine. Once Damien was safely inside, it was Dalton's turn. Tippy joined Dalton under the table and laid his head on Dalton's arms. "Help! Help!" Dalton screeched as he rolled away from the black lab. Carl helped Dalton to his feet and led him to join Damien and Darren in the purple box. By this time, the gingerbread man had gotten off Barrett's chest and Tippy was guarding him, growling fiercely. Carl came over and pulled Barrett to his feet.

Barrett scowled at the gingerbread man and snarled, "How'd you do that?"

"You should never underestimate a gingerbread man," Samuel replied as he held out his right hand toward me. "Hand me the blue candy flower that Carl gave you in the meadow, Sam."

I fished around in my pocket until I found the budding blue candy. I handed it to the gingerbread man as he requested. As soon as the candy touched his hand, the gingerbread man crumpled into a heap of crumbs on the floor. Tippy sniffed at the crumbs and as soon as his nose touched the little heap of remnants of the doughy cookie, a green light flashed from the machine. Samuel stood where the cookie man had crumpled.

Barrett's eyes grew large, and he swallowed several times before he gasped, "How'd you do that?"

"Come on, young man. We've wasted enough time," Samuel ignored the question as he shoved Barrett into the waiting machine. Carl used the remaining strap to secure him to the chair.

Samuel brushed the crumbs from his pants as he joined Mrs. Lawrence outside the machine. "I'm getting too old for this," he joked as he slipped his arm around her waist.

"You'll never be too old," she responded brushing the hair back from his forehead.

Carl closed the door to his invention.

Turning to Samuel, Mrs. Lawrence whispered, "Would you like to do the honors, Dear?"

"Who, me?" he quipped. The two joined hands, whispered some words I couldn't quite make out, and vanished.

The whirring sound from Carl's invention filled the basement. The lights flashed four times before turning green. Tippy, standing by the door of the weird machine, let out a triumphant bark. Carl opened the door and out staggered Dalton, Barrett, Darren, and Damien. Tippy took one look at the emerging boys, yelped once, raced across the basement, and scrambled up the stairs. I wondered why Tippy was running from the boys when he hadn't before. The answer wasn't long in coming.

"Nice try, but it didn't work," snarled Barrett as he advanced toward me, his eyes narrowed. He clenched his teeth so tightly that the muscles bulged along his jaw. "Thought you got rid of us, didn't you?" It wasn't Barrett, but the familiar in possession of Barrett's body, who was threatening me.

Dalton turned on Carl and backed him into the EATT machine until his legs pressed against the leather chair. "How'd you like a dose of your own medicine? Get in that chair, pretty boy. You're going on a journey into the past. Threaten to turn us into dogs, will you?" Darren and Damien went to help Dalton secure Carl in the padded chair.

Carl swung his right fist at Dalton's face. The blow caught Dalton off guard, and he fell to his knees, but the other two familiars overpowered Carl easily. They secured him to the chair and gave each other a high five and started dancing around the chair and its captive.

What had gone wrong? Why were the familiars still here? Where were Samuel and Mrs. Lawrence? What could I do now? I really didn't know how to control my power so how was I going to vanquish these familiars? Maybe we *should* have turned them into dogs.

I glared at Barrett as he continued advancing. I narrowed my eyes and concentrated on Barrett's eyes.

Without warning, a small fog-like mist arose from Barrett's head and swirled lightly toward the ceiling. I didn't blink as I held Barrett's eyes with mine. As the mist rose toward the ceiling, Barrett's body dropped heavily to the basement floor, and a poodle wearing a pink tutu and blue ribbons tied around its neck pranced across Barrett's inert form.

Dalton, on his hands and knees facing me, saw the change in his friend, and his eyes widened so far that I thought they would pop out of his head. He opened his mouth to scream, but the sound caught in his throat as his eyes locked with mine. Once again, I narrowed my eyes and watched in amazement as the fog-like mist rose from Dalton and his body dropped to the floor in a heap. A Chihuahua sporting a yellow tutu and orange ribbons flounced around the fallen boy.

Darren and Damien finished their victory dance and turned to find their two companions lying limply on the cold cement floor. They saw the two dogs prancing around the limp forms of their friends. Their eyes drifted upward and widened as they saw the two fog-like clouds floating near the ceiling. They looked back at me and their mouths gaped open.

"Who's next? I feel like creating a toad or two. Would you care to volunteer? Darren? Damien?" I glared at the two remaining familiars without blinking.

Damien shrugged his shoulders as he sat on the threshold of the EATT machine. His eyes never left mine. "Go ahead. At least I won't have as far to fall." The mist began rising from Damien and his body slumped against the doorframe as a toad wearing glasses hopped into the machine. Darren reached out and tugged at the mist as it floated past his head. The mist stopped rising and hovered just above Darren's head.

Darren raised his eyes to the ceiling and whistled loudly. The two fog-like clouds began to descend and hovered near the one already at Darren's head. "Gotta jar, Sam? I might as well help you catch them since you removed them from their hosts. Don't worry. I won't do anythin' stupid. I know when I can't win." Darren's voice sounded hoarse.

Carl spoke for the first time since the familiars had overpowered him. "Look under the sink, Sam. You should find some jars there. But first untie me so I can help you."

Quickly, I undid the straps that Damien and Darren had used to secure Carl to the chair. Meanwhile, Darren had moved toward the sink with the three fog-like shapes hovering over him like dust clouds. He took four jars off the shelf and removed the lids from three of them. Each time he removed a lid, one of the hovering shapes swirled into the jar. Darren replaced the lids and gently set the jars in the machine. He handed the final jar to me after he removed the top. As soon as the jar touched my hand, Darren's body collapsed at my feet as the foggy mist that left him entered the jar. A black snake slithered into the machine. I set the final jar in the leather chair.

Carl rounded up the two dancing dogs and placed them in the EATT machine with the bespectacled toad and the snake. He dragged Damien's limp body to the floor beside Barrett's. I grabbed Dalton's feet and Carl lifted him under the arms. We dragged him from the machine.

Carl secured the door and twisted a knob. The now familiar whirring sound filled the basement. Once again, the lights flashed four times before turning green. Carl opened the door. This time, the machine was empty.

At out feet, the four boys began to stir restlessly as they regained consciousness. The boys' eyes grew to three times their normal size as they gazed around the basement. Their mouths were hanging open as they turned in a circle and discovered the vat in one corner and the strange looking machine behind them.

Darren, the first to recover sufficiently to move, turned to Carl. Before he could speak, Carl said quietly, "It's late. Let's go upstairs."

"Where are we?" Darren managed to mutter. "I don' recognize this place."

"Upstairs," Carl insisted leading the way across the room. Tippy, head down, tail between his legs, greeted us at the top of the stairs.

In the living room, Carl leaned against the mantle. "Have a seat on the couch, guys."

Damien could barely keep his eyes open, while Dalton yawned loudly. Barrett's head fell forward and he jerked upright. Darren hid a yawn behind his hand. Just when I thought all four would fall asleep, Mrs. Lawrence arrived jingling her car keys.

It took Carl and me four trips from the living room to the garage to get our groggy classmates tucked safely in Mrs. Lawrence's van. Once we had them settled, I got in the front seat with Mrs. Lawrence and Carl rode in the back. We dropped each boy off at his own home.

Carl tapped Mrs. Lawrence on the shoulder. "Won't those guys cause problems when they remember what happened tonight?"

Mrs. Lawrence signaled for the turn into my street. "The last thing any of them will recall will be walking out of the skating rink to sneak a smoke."

"Are they goin' to be themselves again?" Carl asked from the back as he leaned forward over the seat.

"Unfortunately, yes," Mrs. Lawrence answered as she parked the van in front of my house. "And the familiars are safely in the past, where they belong. They shouldn't cause any more trouble."

Carl got out of the van and opened the van door for me. I stepped down.

"Good night, Mrs. Lawrence," we said at the same time.

"Good night, kids. Get a good night's sleep. Try to be at my house by nine in the morning. We have some unfinished business to take care of."

Carl grabbed my arm and whirled me around to face him.

"Sam, how did you change those familiars into other shapes?"

"I don't know how I did it. I just glared at them the way I glared at you when you turned into a butterfly, and they changed."

"Then you weren't joking when you said you turned me into a butterfly? I don't remember it." Carl squeezed my hand as he continued, "Remind me not to make you mad."

13
Doubts

Carl stood on the sidewalk while I let myself into the house through a small window in the basement. Once inside, I turned to wave at Carl so he would know I was safe. He waved back and trotted off across the street to his own home. I closed the little window, but didn't lock it in case I might need to use it again sometime.

I crept silently up the basement steps to the ground floor. The door opened into the kitchen and I listened until I was positive no one waited for me on the other side. I pushed my way into the deserted kitchen and opened the refrigerator as silently as possible. Aunt Kate had put some roast beef, left over from supper, in a covered plastic dish. I helped myself to a couple of slices and made myself a quick sandwich. I didn't put any mayo on it because I knew if I turned the water on to rinse the knife, the old pipes in the house would groan, knock, and probably wake someone. I didn't want to get caught sneaking into the house. If my aunt or uncle woke and asked me where I'd been, I couldn't lie to them, and they sure wouldn't believe me if I told them the truth.

I tiptoed to the foot of the big staircase in the hall without incident. The challenge was reaching the second floor without stepping on the individual steps that invariably creaked when anyone used them. For some strange reason, they only squeaked when someone went up the stairs, not down. Cautiously I began my journey, avoiding the third step by skipping it completely and pulling myself up the banister with my right hand. I continued climbing, avoiding the sixth and tenth steps in the same manner. I had reached the top of the stairs when I heard the toilet flush in the guest bathroom and the water gurgle in the old pipes.

The bathroom is directly across the hall from the stairs and I knew if I didn't move, whoever came out of that room would see me. Could I make it to my room before the door opened? Should I stay here and risk someone seeing me?

My room was at the end of the hall, but maybe I could make it to the large walk-in closet to the left of where I stood. I darted quickly for the closet and had just eased the door most of the way closed when a beam of light fell across the hall floor. I peeked out the slight opening and saw Kate, looking like a ghost in her long white nightgown. Breathing a small inaudible sigh of relief, I relaxed. Aunt Kate, without her glasses, couldn't see two feet away clearly.

I waited until the guest room door closed behind my aunt before leaving the safety of the closet and slipping down the hall to my own room. Once inside, I felt my way to my bedside table, put my sandwich down, and turned on the lamp. I stifled a scream as I turned toward the bed and saw the lump under the blankets. It looked like someone was in my bed. My heart hammered in my chest as I hesitantly reached out to pull back the blanket only to reveal two pillows covered to resemble the shape of a person. Who could have done that? When could someone have placed the pillows there, and why?

I wasn't going to get any answers tonight, so I sat on the edge of my bed and ate my sandwich. Glancing at the clock on my bedside table, I saw that it was just after one in the morning. I changed into my PJ's and lay down to get a few hours sleep.

I tried to sleep but my mind kept racing. I couldn't shake the image of how I had looked in the mirror. Why did I turn blue and have all those ugly yellow warts when the green light hit the drawing? Why didn't anything happen to Carl? Was Samuel really my great-great grandfather? How did Mrs. Lawrence fit into all this? The questions kept coming, causing me to toss and turn for over an hour. Finally, I turned the lamp back on and reached for my diary. Maybe I could get it out of my system by writing it down. Maybe it would make a little sense then. I couldn't locate my pen in the drawer of the nightstand so I got out of bed and padded over to the dresser in my bare feet. Was the door with its brass knob still there? Had I imagined everything?

I tried to see behind the dresser but it was so close to the wall that I couldn't tell if the dented brass doorknob was there. I hurried back to my bedside table and found my flashlight. I had to know if the door existed or if

I was having a dream. I shined the light between the wall and the dresser. I had to look really hard, but there, about eighteen inches above the floor I could make out the faint gleam of brass.

It is true. I am a witch and I have magic powers. How do I use them? Do I just wave my hand and say some weird words? What if I changed someone into say, a monkey, and couldn't change them back? Carl and Mrs. Lawrence have magic powers too. When were they going to tell me? What did Mrs. Lawrence mean about the others? She never did answer that question.

I grabbed a pen off the dresser and scurried back to the warmth of my bed to record the evening's events in my diary. I didn't want to forget anything.

I must have drifted off because the next thing I knew the alarm was sounding. I pushed the button down to get a few more minutes of sleep. Five minutes later when the alarm went off again, I reached out to hit snooze and suddenly sat upright in the bed. I couldn't sleep now! Today was going to be a busy day.

I'm a witch. A real witch! If I'm a witch, why don't I feel any different? Do I look different? I jumped out of bed and ran to my dresser. The image gazing back at me from the mirror had long reddish brown hair and a straight nose. The teeth were white, and the few freckles sprinkled across the bridge of my nose were hardly noticeable against my skin. I tilted my head back and twirled around enjoying the silky feel of my hair as it brushed my skin. I sighed deeply and smiled at my reflection. Sam, you are so dumb. Did you expect to see a monster of some kind? Get yourself together, girl. Get some clothes on and let's go. As Uncle Art would say, "Time's a wastin'."

14
Carl's Story

As I dressed, the aroma of sausage cooking drifted into my room and made my tummy growl. Aunt Kate had breakfast ready when I got downstairs. I didn't want to risk upsetting her after the way I had disappeared yesterday, so I humored her and had a plate of pancakes and sausage. While we were eating Kate said, "Did you sleep well? You sure went to bed early last night. I looked in on you around ten and you had the blanket up over your head. I turned your light off."

"I slept ok, I guess. When I got home around nine thirty, your car wasn't here, so I went up to my room to read. I didn't intend to go to bed early," I replied with my mouth full of her delicious buttermilk pancakes. "I don't know what happened. I lay down for a few minutes and the next thing I knew, it was morning." I kept my fingers crossed in the childish way that I always did when I wasn't telling the truth. I had better distract her. "Oh, I found my bracelet under the bed."

Kate's eyebrows raised a little as she looked at me. Did she know I was lying? She tilted her head to the right as she studied me. Maybe she realized my hair isn't quite the same.

"Nine thirty? Then you just missed us. Art decided that he wanted some ice cream, so we ran down to the grocery store," Kate replied. "I knew you would find your bracelet somewhere. Sam, what did you do to your hair? I don't recall it being that shade of brown."

"Carl's mom put some red highlights in it yesterday afternoon. She said it was an early Christmas present and if I don't like it, she can cover the highlights and make me look like me again. I really like it. What do you think?" Under the table, I now had my fingers crossed on both hands.

She studied my hair some more. "Turn around and let me see the back."

I stood up and spun in a circle slowly so she could get the full effect.

"I like it, too. Did she trim the ends?"

"Yeah. Carl's mom is taking classes to be a beautician and sometimes she needs someone to practice on."

"Oh, that's right. I think she told me about her classes a couple of weeks ago. Well, she certainly did a good job. Maybe she'll fix my hair sometime," Kate pulled a strand of her honey-blonde hair in front of her face and examined it.

I continued eating. I hadn't told a complete lie. Carl's mom was taking classes so she could open a beauty shop at home. She did experiment with my hair sometimes, just not yesterday. Kate's voice interrupted my musing.

"What are your plans for today? We can go Christmas shopping later if you want to. I need to stop by my house, too, and water the plants."

"I'd love to go shopping with you. But if it's ok with you, can we do it this afternoon? Carl and I have a project due in science next week, and we're goin' to work on it this mornin'," I responded as I shoveled the last of the pancakes into my mouth.

"Is two o'clock okay?"

"Sure," I answered, kissing my aunt on the cheek and grabbing my jacket. "I gotta meet Carl. I'll see you at two," I called, putting the jacket on as I reached the front door.

Carl met me when I emerged from my house at eight thirty. The temperature outside hovered around thirty-five degrees, and we had dressed warmly. We had gone only a few steps when he began to explain some things to me.

"Sam, you've probably guessed by now that I also have some magic powers. They aren't as strong as yours are, but I'm workin' on that. What happened yesterday was partially my fault. I knew someone was following us, but I wasn't sure who. I should have paid more attention to what was happenin' around us. Those four bullies should never have gotten that close to you." He paused as two kids on bikes passed us.

I smiled up at him. "They wouldn't have gotten that close to me if you'd gone through the door first."

Carl blushed. "Yeah, well, I don't like to admit it, Sam, but when it comes to magic powers, you're stronger than me."

I took a little skipping step to keep up with his longer stride. "Thanks for the vote of confidence, but I sure didn't feel that strong."

Carl shortened his stride and turned to look at my face. "You know, Sam, you were kinda cute with those yellow warts. I kinda liked the twisted one on the tip of your balloon nose." He wiggled his forefinger at me, as if he was going to put a spell on me. "Would you like to have them back?"

I punched his right arm, and he laughed, "Just kiddin', Sam. I really like you better the way you are now."

"You're not so bad yourself, Carl," I joked.

We walked along in a companionable silence for a while until finally Carl resumed his story.

"I've known about my powers for about six months. The night I found a small door behind the stereo in my room, I nearly freaked out. That's when I met Tiny and Samuel. Only for me there wasn't a candy garden, but a zoo. My contact wasn't a gingerbread man, but a talking giraffe. If you thought talking to a cookie was weird, you should try talking to a giraffe. I had a crick in my neck for three days from looking up at 'im."

I laughed. "I remember when that happened. You told me you had hurt your neck while practicin' for the skateboarding tournament."

He nodded. "Yeah, well I didn't think you'd believe the truth. Shucks, I hardly believed it myself. Sometimes I still wonder if it really happened."

We walked along in silence for a minute. Carl kicked a pebble that was lying on the sidewalk. "I was trying to change a kitten into a lion when Mrs. Lawrence caught me. It's probably a good thing she came into the lab when she did. I hadn't thought about how dangerous a lion could be." Carl laughed. "That lady really is remarkable, Sam. You won't believe what she can do. She knows all this scientific stuff an' she lets me use her basement for my experiments." Carl was grinning from ear to ear. He loved his experiments almost as much as he loved his skateboard.

"OK, Carl. I get the message. Mrs. Lawrence is the greatest," I rolled my eyes at him.

Carl blushed. "Sorry, Sam. I guess I got carried away, huh?" He shrugged his shoulders. "Anyway, last month we learned from Samuel about the scheme to take over this town. I knew you were a witch, even though you hadn't discovered it yet. Samuel knew that you would need my help, so he sorta let that secret about you slip out. Apparently, the familiars knew it, too." Carl stopped walking and turned to me. "Sam, you and I aren't the only ones in this town who have magical powers. Tara and Jasmine are also witches, but it turns out that their powers are even weaker than mine, so they couldn't be of much help."

Wait a minute. Two of my best friends were witches and they hadn't told me? How long had they known? Just wait 'til I see them again.

"We got Haley to help us." I stopped walking and stared at Carl. He grinned sheepishly. "Yeah, Haley is a witch, too." This was too much. Haley was a witch, too? And she hadn't told me? How many more of my classmates had traveled to the candy garden or whatever they found on the other side of the small door? Was everyone in town a witch?

As if reading my mind, Carl went on, "There are five of us, Sam. Tara and Jasmine only found out about their powers two days ago, so they weren't too helpful. However, Haley has known for two months, and her magic is almost as strong as yours is. She went through her door to get some information for her report on the Roarin' Twenties. While she was doin' her research, she overheard some talk about kidnappin' you so you couldn't interfere with the plan to control the town." Carl kicked the pebble again. "The rebels thought if you were out of the picture, they would be able to succeed. Somehow, they knew that you would be strong enough, or smart enough, to defeat them. Haley told Samuel what she had learned, and he told me. That's when I knew that you were the one we needed to help us outwit the rebellin' familiars. Samuel said that you had to come to us. We couldn't just ask you to help. 'Specially when you didn't know about your ability." Carl grinned.

"Then, there you were, standing on the sidewalk, lookin' like an escapee from a horror film, and I knew that you had opened your small door. And, as they say, the rest is history."

Carl had probably never said so much at one time in his life. I had the feeling he was holding something back, but I wasn't sure what it was. By the time Carl had finished his story, we were standing outside Mrs. Lawrence's front gate. Tippy was waiting for us and promptly jumped up on Carl and knocked him flat. A laugh from the front door let us know that the science teacher also waited for us. Carl got up and brushed himself off sheepishly.

15
A Legacy

"He does that to me ever' time," Carl laughed as he bent over to pet the frisky black lab. We scurried up the walkway to the front porch.

"Come on in, kids. Samuel and I have been waiting for you," she greeted us. "You're just in time to say goodbye to him. He has to leave soon, but he has some information for you first."

Samuel sat at the kitchen table buttering a slice of toast. When he saw us, he stood and bowed deeply. "Good morning. I've been learning about some of your new-fangled machines. We never imagined back in my day that someday people could turn on a machine and have the world just a click away. Nor did we imagine putting food in a box and heating it in just seconds. This is a fascinating time to live in. Civilization has surely advanced, and I'm almost sorry I can't be here to enjoy all these changes. However, I must get back to my own life. Before I go, Samantha, I must tell you about your legacy."

We had all taken seats at the kitchen table as he spoke. Mrs. Lawrence had placed a couple of glasses of orange juice in front of Carl and me. Samuel reached across the table and took my right hand in his own.

"We all know that what happened yesterday and early this morning was the direct result of witchcraft." He glanced at Carl as he spoke. "No one is at fault. Yes, Carl, I know you blame yourself because you spilled the liquid from the vat on that old photograph. It was just a coincidence that Samantha discovered her unique little door at the same moment. She would have become aware of her gift eventually. You had nothing to do with what happened to Sam."

Carl grinned as he picked up his glass. "You mean I didn't cause Sam any trouble? Whew! That's a load off my mind."

"Well, Carl may not have caused me any trouble, but somebody sure kept me out of trouble last night," I remarked just as Carl put his glass to his lips.

Carl put his glass down without tasting the juice and leaned toward me. "What'ya mean? What kind of trouble?"

Casually, I lifted my juice glass to my lips and took a sip of the cold liquid. I deliberately delayed answering Carl's questions as long as I could. I said in a small voice, "Kate trouble."

"Kate trouble? What in the world are you talkin' about? How could you have Kate trouble? Did she catch you sneakin' back in when we dropped you off? You're not grounded or anythin', are you?"

Mrs. Lawrence's shoulders shook with laughter and Samuel chuckled as Carl's frown deepened. He looked from Mrs. Lawrence's face to Samuel's and then to mine. Finally, he grinned as he caught on to what I was talking about.

"Oh." He looked at me, his eyes gleaming. "Kate trouble. Now I understand. She looked in on you last night, didn't she?" He nodded his head, answering his own question.

"Yeah, she did. About ten o'clock. And I was fast asleep under the covers." I started to giggle. "Only I wasn't and we all know it."

"Nope. You were on the other side of the door with me and Samuel. So why did Kate think it was you under the cover?"

"I think I can clear that up for you," Mrs. Lawrence replied. "Tippy and I were waiting for you to return with the gingerbread man when we heard a noise in the hallway. Tippy hid behind the dresser and I stuffed those two pillows under your blanket." She sipped her coffee. "I waited in the closet until your aunt closed the door after checking on you and turning off the lamp by your bed. When I heard your aunt's bedroom door close, I turned on the desk lamp and told Tippy to make sure you found my note. Then, I snuck downstairs and out the unlocked window in the basement that you and Carl use when you don't want anyone to see you. I guess you didn't see the lump in your bed earlier because Tippy kept you distracted. You went to your desk, read the note, and found a disguise for the gingerbread man, all without going near your bed."

"Good thinking, my dear," Samuel commented as he took another sip of his coffee and leaned back in his chair. He turned to me and his smile grew dimmer. "Back to the business of your gift, Samantha. We've been calling your powers a gift, but they could be a curse. You're the only one who will make that decision. You can be a good witch, or you can be a bad witch. There will be times when you are tempted to use your magic to change things, but you must be very careful. Your powers are not a toy. You cannot take them lightly, nor use them capriciously. And remember, not everyone understands witchcraft, and what people don't understand, they fear. And what they fear, they often try to destroy."

"How will I know if I should use my powers?" I asked as he paused to take another sip of coffee.

"You'll know," he promised me. "I've been watching over you since you were an infant. I know that you seldom act without thinking things through. You do ask plenty of questions, but that's a good thing for someone in your situation. In addition, you succeeded in using your witchcraft without guidance last night when you handled those familiars the way you did." He patted my hand. "I know we should have warned you that the machine wouldn't send the familiars away as long as they were in possession of your friends' bodies. However, Mrs. Lawrence and I wanted to see how you would use your powers. We would have stepped in if you had needed us, but you rose to the occasion quite well." He pushed his chair back from the table. "Two dogs, a toad, and a snake, a most imaginative way of handling things. You see, Samantha, you're a witch whether you want to believe it or not. There is no changing that fact, no escaping the truth, no denying your destiny and your legacy. It won't be easy for you, but if you have any doubts, you can always come to this house. If this woman, whom you know as Mrs. Lawrence, can't help you, she knows how to reach me. We will do our best to guide you in the right direction."

"How do you know what happened in the basement after you left? You did leave, didn't you?" I looked from Samuel to Mrs. Lawrence.

Samuel glanced at Mrs. Lawrence before answering my questions. She gave him a slight nod, and he continued, "We never left you alone with those familiars. Mrs. Lawrence simply removed us from your view." He chuckled, "We waited in the shadows near the vat to see how you would handle the situation. And handle it, you did. You not only got the familiars to leave their hosts' bodies, but you created two charming, if ridiculous looking, dancing dogs, a toad, and a black snake. Not bad, for an amateur."

Carl leaned his chair back on two legs. "Sam was awesome. The way she stood up to those familiars and didn't back down. Man, I'm glad I wasn't the target of that look." He shuddered melodramatically. "I could just imagine me as one of those silly dancing dogs cavorting all over the basement. Yuck!"

I couldn't resist. "No, Carl. For you, it would have to be something special. How about the neck of a giraffe, the body of a yappy little Chihuahua, and the head of a cow?" I giggled at the absurdity of the picture created by my comment. Carl's chair legs hit the floor with a thud.

Samuel chuckled again as he reminded me, "Use your powers wisely, Samantha. No matter how tempting it may be to TEMISE Carl, save your energy for a better use."

"TEMISE?" Carl and I asked simultaneously.

"Yes," laughed Mrs. Lawrence. "That's what we call what you did to those familiars. It means transforming energy matter into something else. TEMISE."

"I guess I do have a lot to learn. I never heard that term before. I did it, but I didn't know it had a name."

Mrs. Lawrence added, "Yes, Carl and you both have much to learn. You'll need guidance to use your powers properly, but if you come here every Saturday morning at ten o'clock, I'll teach you what you need to know. Carl has already started strengthening his powers, but perhaps you can help him become even stronger. You see, his powers come from an ancestor accused of witchcraft in 1419 in England. Over time, the powers have weakened from lack of use. Both of you need to practice using your powers. My basement is the perfect place to hone your skills."

I spun my empty juice glass on the table, making a kaleidoscope pattern with the wet circles. How could Mrs. Lawrence help me learn witchcraft? Wasn't she a mortal? No, Samuel told me Mrs. Lawrence has powers too. He also said she would tell me when she's ready.

I set the glass in the middle of the circular design. "Mrs. Lawrence, why didn't you go with Carl and me through the small door?"

Tears sprang to Mrs. Lawrence's eyes and Samuel covered her hand with his. He cleared his throat. "Do you remember that I told you not to remove that dented brass doorknob?"

"Yes, but what would happen if I did remove it?"

Samuel wasn't looking at me as he replied. He was gazing at Mrs. Lawrence as he said sadly, "You would be stuck in time."

What did he mean by that? Stuck in time? How could anyone get stuck in time? It seems like every time I get an answer, three more questions pop up.

I looked from Samuel to Mrs. Lawrence. "Stuck in time?"

Mrs. Lawrence wiped her eyes. "It's a long story, Sam. I'll explain after Samuel leaves."

Samuel wiped his mouth with a napkin. "Now, it's time for me to go."

"Wait! Before you go, can you, er, will you answer some questions for me?" I interrupted.

"I'll try," he responded glancing quickly at Mrs. Lawrence.

"What do you want to know, Samantha?" Mrs. Lawrence put her hand on Samuel's.

"Well, I know I turned into the image I drew in first grade when Tiny's light hit the drawing. I'd like to know *why*."

Carl laughed heartily. "I wondered when you'd ask about the way you looked."

Samuel chuckled as he warned Carl, "Be nice, Carl. After all, she has more power than you do." Then he turned to me. "Samantha, when you stepped through the small door the first time, you activated a curse that the Witches' Council had placed on your door at my mother's request. She had it placed there to discourage any female offspring from engaging in witchcraft. That curse turned you into your idea of what a witch looks like. The fact that you had that picture of a witch on your bed in plain sight when Tiny arrived made it easier. The curse went into effect when the green light from the other side illuminated the drawing."

"Hey, Sam, you could even say that you made yourself look like you did. You put a curse on yourself and didn't even know it." Carl had to add his unwanted opinion. Well, he'd better watch out. Someday he might find himself on the receiving end of one of my curses. The thought made me giggle as I once again pictured

Carl with a giraffe's neck, a yappy dog's body, and the head of a cow. That would show him a thing or two.

Samuel covered my hand with his. "You could've reversed the curse yourself by stepping through the door a second time."

I glared at Carl. "Why didn't Carl tell me that instead of dragging me to Mrs. Lawrence's basement?"

Carl shrugged. "By then, it was too late. Once you stepped out your front door and the cold air hit your skin, stepping back through the door wouldn't have helped."

My eyes narrowed. "So you're tellin' me I would have been normal again if I had just gone back to the candy garden?"

Carl grinned and winked at me. "Yeah. But think of all the fun you would've missed." I kicked his leg under the table.

While Carl was rubbing his leg, I turned back to Samuel. "Why didn't anything happen to Carl?" I demanded. "He hadn't been through that door before."

"You're right. However, he had been through the one in his own room. All witches have one so that they can travel freely into the past. Not all doors are in the same place, but all of them have the dented brass doorknob.

"I really do have to go now. Don't forget, Carl and you must both be very careful when using witchcraft. Trust Mrs. Lawrence. She's not really the mean teacher that your friends say she is."

Samuel stood up. Carl shook his hand. I gave him a hug. Then he and Mrs. Lawrence once again joined hands and whispered words I couldn't quite make out. Both vanished.

16
Stuck in Time

"Carl, how do Samuel and Mrs. Lawrence know each other? They seem to be real friendly."

"I'm not really sure, but I think that Samuel and our Mrs. Lawrence are sweet on each other. Did you notice that ever' time they join hands, they somehow manage to disappear? I wonder where they go."

"That is really none of your business," Mrs. Lawrence's soft voice said from the vicinity of the open kitchen door.

Carl and I looked around the kitchen. There was no one else in the room except Tippy and the two of us. Carl bent over and peered under the table.

"Did you say that, Sam?" Carl inquired as he straightened up. "Are you already practicin' your magic?"

"Nah, it wasn't me! I didn't do a thing," I replied.

"No, Carl. Samantha didn't say it. I did." Mrs. Lawrence's voice had moved to the table. A chair moved backward with a loud scraping sound. "Sit down, and I'll tell you a little more about my past."

As we seated ourselves at the table, I could make out a shadowy form in the chair that had moved. The shape became more distinct as Mrs. Lawrence materialized in the chair.

"How did you do that?" Carl and I asked simultaneously.

"You'll learn soon enough," Mrs. Lawrence actually laughed. "Now do you want to hear my story or not?"

Once again, Carl and I spoke in unison. "Tell us!"

"Okay. It all started in 1907. I met Samuel two years before his mother died. He and I got along splendidly from the very beginning. Four years to the day after we met, Samuel and I got married. Samuel's magical powers were dormant, but mine were active." Mrs. Lawrence's voice dropped to almost a whisper. She leaned toward us. "I was, and still am, a witch. A very powerful witch. I used my witchcraft to give Samuel the power to travel into, and see the future. The Witches' Council punished me by sending me into the future and keeping Samuel in the past. The Witches' Council removed the brass doorknob. That's why I can never go back through any magical doors to other realms. He can visit as often as he wants, but every time he travels into the future, he ages six months. After the Council banished me, Samuel had to raise our two sons on his own. The oldest of those boys was Samantha's great grandfather."

Carl's eyes opened wide and his mouth formed a perfect O. My face mirrored his. I could almost hear the gears click in his head as he let the teacher's words filter to his brain. "That means that you're Sam's great-great gran'mother, doesn't it? Wow! This is totally unreal. Can you believe it, Sam? Mrs. Lawrence is your great-great gran'mother. I know your last name is Laurence, but I never would've thought there was any relationship. Can you beat that?" He paused for a moment, staring at Mrs. Lawrence as the gears continued to turn. "You don't look like a great-great gran'mother."

"And I never will," Mrs. Lawrence informed him. "When I relocated into the future, I had to remain the same age forever. Of course, this means that I must move every thirty years or so because if I stay in a place too long, someone might realize that I never age. Samuel and I manage to see each other occasionally, but never for very long."

"Don't you get lonely?" I asked.

"Well, I used to. Then I moved to this town, and that all changed. The first time I saw you in the hallway at school, Sam, I knew you were my great-great granddaughter. You look exactly like Samuel's mother. I wanted so badly to tell you, but I couldn't until you discovered your heritage on your own. If I had, then the Witches' Council would have sent me away again. I wasn't about to lose you, so I said nothing, but I've watched you and waited for this time to come."

"Why didn't Samuel tell me?"

"He couldn't either. We both had to wait. Now, with the powers you possess, once you learn to use them properly, you can travel back through the small door to see Samuel whenever you want. He is looking forward to your visits." Mrs. Lawrence smiled at us. "But first you must learn to use your gift to help others. Are you ready for your first lesson, Sam?"

The sound of the front doorbell ringing interrupted her. Mrs. Lawrence glanced at her wristwatch. "I believe the rest of the group has arrived. Carl, would you answer the door, please?"

"Sure, Mrs. L." Carl jumped up from the table and left the kitchen. A minute later, he returned followed by Tara, Jasmine, and Haley. Now I knew what she meant by the rest of the group. These were the other girls that Carl had told me were witches. Not only were they witches, they were also members of our girls' softball team, the Winfield Spirits.

I stood as they entered the kitchen, and Haley rushed over to hug me. Haley is my age but most people think she is at least two years older. She towers over me by about eight inches. And boy, is she fast on her feet. Her mouth is almost as fast as her feet. Haley talks a mile a minute, as Uncle Art is fond of saying.

The words flowed from Haley's mouth like white water rapids. "So you finally know the truth! Isn't it great? Just think of all the magic we can do together. I can hardly wait to get started. Hello, Mrs. Lawrence. Are we early? I know you said to be here at ten, so here we are." Did Haley ever take a breath? Sometimes it made me tired just to listen to her.

Tara was the captain of our softball team. Although she didn't look very athletic with her long blonde hair and willowy build, she could throw a no-hitter game four times out of five. She always told me she didn't need to look like a guy to play like one.

Jasmine, our catcher, was the athletic-looking one. Her dark brown eyes sparkled as she greeted the science teacher, "Hey, Mrs. Lawrence. Haley said you wanted to see us this mornin'. What's happenin'?"

"Good morning, girls. Thanks for being so punctual. I asked you here because you all have something in common beyond the ordinary. You all found out recently that you're witches. Each of you possesses at least one magical talent that you must learn to utilize to the fullest. I can let you stumble along on your own, or I can help you become responsible witches. The choice is yours."

Haley nodded vigorously as Mrs. Lawrence finished speaking. "I've already had a few witchcraft lessons from Mrs. Lawrence. She helped me find my special talent. I'm gonna keep comin' back as long as she can help me develop my skills."

Tara, who had only discovered her heritage two days earlier, licked her lips nervously before she spoke. "This is all so new to me. You say I'm a witch, but I don't feel any different than I did before I found that little door with the brass doorknob behind the headboard of my bed. If you can help me develop my powers, then I'll be here for lessons."

Mrs. Lawrence smiled as Tara removed her coat and hung it on the back of one of the kitchen chairs. "Good. Now, Jasmine, what about you? Are you willing to give up your Saturday mornings so that you can learn to control your power?"

Jasmine removed her jacket and hung it on top of Tara's. "I'll give it a shot. After all, what good is it to have power and not know how to use it?"

Mrs. Lawrence nodded. "Sam, will you join us on Saturdays?"

I grinned. "Count me in. I wouldn't miss it for anythin'."

"Well, that's settled. Come on to the basement so we can get started on your first lesson."

As Mrs. Lawrence led the way to the basement, a sudden thought occurred to me. What do I call a great-great grandmother who looks like she is thirty-five years old? What do I call a great-great grandmother who teaches me science? What do I call a great-great grandmother who is a witch? I couldn't call her Granny. She didn't look like one. I couldn't call her Grandma because I already had one. I could call her Mrs. Lawrence, but that sounded too formal.

Sensing my dilemma, my great-great grandmother put her smooth hand on mine and said in a low musical voice, "Don't worry, Sam. We'll think of something you can call me later. For now, continue to call me Mrs. Lawrence. We don't need everyone at school knowing that we have a special relationship."

"We know, but we won't tell anyone," Tara flipped her long blonde hair back from her face. "We know it's a secret. I just love secrets, don't you Jasmine?"

Jasmine looked around the basement as if seeing it for the first time. "Secret? Who has a secret?"

"Pay attention, Jasmine. You know we're talkin' about Mrs. Lawrence bein' Sam's great-great grandmother," Tara tapped Jasmine on her black cornrows. "You are so thick-headed sometimes. I don't know why I put up with you."

"Thick-headed? At least I'm not an airhead," Jasmine retorted as she pulled a lock of Tara's bleached blonde hair.

"Can't you two ever be serious? Sam has a problem, and we need to help her. How would you feel if suddenly you discovered that your science teacher was your great-great grandmother?" Haley crossed her arms over her chest as she chided her two friends. "How would you feel if you found out that you are a witch?" Suddenly she giggled. "Oops! I forgot, we're all witches. How cool is that? Here we are best friends and all of us are witches."

"When do I get my magic broom? Don't all witches have a magic broom that they ride across the moon?" Jasmine pretended to fly around the basement room where we had come to learn some control of our magical powers. She bumped into the ping-pong table and knocked the ball to the floor. The hollow sound it made as it bounced away from her filled the sudden silence in the room.

Mrs. Lawrence frowned as she looked at Jasmine running around on her "broom". "Sit down, Jasmine. Being a witch is a serious matter, not something to treat lightly. If you're not willing to learn the art of magic, and to take it seriously, perhaps you don't belong here."

Jasmine pouted as she found a seat at a table that was near the EATT machine. "I'm sorry. This is all so new to me. Sometimes I think if I pinch myself, I'll wake up in my own bed, and all of this," she glanced at the vat in one corner and the EATT machine in the other, "will turn out to be a dream. You gotta admit, it don't seem real."

"It *doesn't* seem real," Mrs. Lawrence automatically corrected Jasmine's grammar. "Don't say 'it don't.' How many times have I told you that?"

Haley grinned at Jasmine. "You gotta tell Jasmine at least once a day. She's so hard-headed."

"Am not," Jasmine argued. "I just don't see no need to use good grammar when I ain't in class."

Mrs. Lawrence's lips twitched at the corners. "But you are in class. Magic class."

"Sorry. I forgot." muttered Jasmine. She pulled a stick of gum from her pocket, removed the wrapper, and dropped it on the floor. She popped the gum in her mouth and began chewing vigorously.

Haley glanced at the gum wrapper on the floor, pointed at it and wiggled her finger. The wrapper started to rise slowly upward until it was directly in front of Jasmine's face. Jasmine's eyes grew wide as she saw the wrapper hanging in front of her. "Whoa! How'd you do that, Haley?"

"If you'd pay attention, you'd know how I did it. In fact, you could have done it yourself. Now take the wrapper, and next time you feel like throwin' your trash on the floor, make sure you're in your own room. This is not a pigpen. We have a purpose for bein' here, and that is to improve our magic skills. Anyone who's not willin' to listen to Mrs. Lawrence, who has so generously donated her Saturdays to helpin' us, needs to leave now and stop wastin' our time." I could tell Haley was serious by the determined set of her jaw. She was almost clenching her teeth as she spoke.

Jasmine pulled her head back like a snake about to strike. "Whoa! Who yanked your chain?"

Haley continued to glare at Jasmine. I halfway expected to see Haley TEMISE Jasmine.

Jasmine yanked the wrapper out of the air. "Okay, okay. I was gonna pick it up anyway. You are so grouchy this morning. Give a girl a break, will you?" Jasmine muttered as she stuffed the offending gum wrapper in the pocket of her tight jeans.

Carl, oblivious of the girls' bickering, wandered over to his EATT machine and started making adjustments on the dials. I could hear him mumbling under his breath as he fiddled with the controls.

Mrs. Lawrence rapped sharply on the table where everyone but Carl had gathered. "That's enough. Jasmine, Haley is right. If you don't want to learn control of your powers, you should leave. I warn you, though, if you choose to go, you could lose your magical ability. The Witches' Council will be keeping a close watch on you and will strip you of your powers if you misuse them or hurt someone when trying to use your powers without guidance. You should know from the beginning that your powers are a gift from someone in the past. Every one of you, except Carl, is a descendant of a Salem witch."

"Does that mean we're all related?" Tara asked wide-eyed.

A small smile played at the corner of Mrs. Lawrence's mouth as she replied:

> *If you do the proper research,*
> *You can find pertinent answers*
> *To the secrets you gained by birth,*
> *And learn more about your ancestors.*

"I didn't know you were a poet." Jasmine popped her gum loudly.

"There is much you don't know about me, but that's not important. What is important is that you learn about the past so that you can understand the present. Now, let's get started on our lesson for today. I must warn you that I'm a tough teacher, but you already know that since all of you are in my classes. I know you've heard what the other students say about me being a witch and being so mean."

Of course, I had heard them say it. I had probably said it at least once myself. However, I knew that from this moment on, whenever I heard one of the other students say anything about Mrs. Lawrence being a witch, I wouldn't be able to deny it. I would just smile and bite my tongue to keep from laughing because now I knew that they were closer to the truth than they would ever know.

17
Return Visit

Carl was still fiddling with his EATT machine an hour later when Mrs. Lawrence ended the magic lesson. He stuck his head out of the machine. "You go on without me, Sam. It'll take me at least ten minutes to fix this circuit."

"Why don't ya just zap it?" Jasmine called across the room.

Carl shook his head. "That takes all the fun out of it. I'm gonna do this the mortal way." He grinned.

I gave him a "thumbs up" signal. "See you later, Carl. Try not to lose track of the time, though. You know your mom wants you to put up the tree this afternoon."

"Don't worry, Sam. I wouldn't miss that for anythin'" Carl waved as the rest of us started up the stairs.

We got our coats from the kitchen and told Mrs. Lawrence we would see her on Monday. At the end of Mrs. Lawrence's sidewalk, Haley and I stopped to say our goodbyes to Jasmine and Tara.

"What're you doin' this afternoon, Sam?" Jasmine asked, pulling her jacket tighter around her neck. "Wanna go Christmas shoppin'? We could meet at my house, and Mom could drive us to the mall." The mall she was talking about was in Newport News about eight miles away.

"I would go with you, Jasmine, but I already promised Kate that I'd go shoppin' with her this afternoon. Maybe I'll see you at the mall," I answered, pulling on my gloves. The air felt colder than it had just two hours before.

"Okay. See you later," Jasmine called as she and Tara turned to the right at the main sidewalk.

"See you later," Tara, Haley, and I simultaneously called out.

"It's gonna snow," I heard Jasmine declare.

"It's not, either." Tara pulled up her hood.

"Sure it is. Those are snow clouds." She pointed to the thick clouds that had rolled in while we practiced improving our magical skills.

"That doesn't mean it's gonna snow," Tara argued back as they walked in the other direction. Haley and I turned left and soon the friendly bickering of the other two was far behind us.

"Are you really going shoppin' with Kate, or was that just an excuse to get away from Jasmine for awhile?" Haley asked as we trudged down the street.

"I promised her we would go shoppin' this afternoon. You mean you think I would make that up so I wouldn't have to go with Jasmine? I wouldn't do somethin' like that," I declared as I lengthened my stride to keep up with Haley.

"Well, maybe you wouldn't 'cause you're just too nice, but sometimes that girl gets on my nerves, and I feel like stranglin' her," Haley replied, shortening her stride a little so I didn't have to practically run to keep up.

I giggled at Haley's reply because I knew exactly how she felt. Although Jasmine meant well, she could be a bit thoughtless at times. I thought that Haley did well to put up with Jasmine's attitude as well as she did.

Haley pushed her sleeve up a little and looked at her watch. "What time are you goin' shoppin'? Do you have time to stop by my house for some lunch?"

"I'd love to stop at your house, but I'd better not. I have a few things I need to do before Kate and I go out." I changed the subject, "Haley, why didn't you tell me when you found out you were a witch?"

"Sam, you will learn that witches don't share that secret with others, 'specially when they think the other person is a mortal. We're secretive, and lookin' back at history, I guess I understand why." Haley waved to a friend in a passing car. "Just look at what happened in Salem when someone accused a neighbor or friend of bein' a witch. We don't want that to happen again, so we keep our witches' heritage a secret."

"I guess I need to study my history so I can understand my own heritage better," I looked at the thickening clouds. "I'll see you later, Haley. Thanks for the lunch offer, but Kate's expectin' me soon."

"See you later, Sam. If I can help you adjust to bein' a witch, just holler. Remember, I've had a little more experience with this than you have," Haley laughed. "At least two months more experience." She waved as she opened her gate and started up the walk. Haley turned back toward me as she called across the sidewalk, "Don't forget to practice your meditatin' for next week's class."

"You're right. I can't forget to do my homework, 'specially for Mrs. Lawrence. She is such a witch."

Haley and I both laughed as she went up the walkway to her front door.

I continued down the sidewalk, my mind racing. Samuel had told me that I was the first active witch in the family since his mother died. Why didn't the males get the witching power, or whatever you called it? Why did it have to be me? I was happy enough being a mortal girl. Why did I have to be a witch? What did witches do? Did they have special groups they met with once or twice a month? How did so many witches end up in one town and why in Winfield? How could I keep my secret from my parents? Did I need to keep it a secret? I wanted to shout to the world, "Look at me, I'm a witch!"

As I entered the front door of my house, I could hear Aunt Kate puttering around in the kitchen. I knew I had made the right decision to come home for lunch when she called out, "Sam, lunch will be ready in thirty minutes."

"Thanks, Aunt Kate. I have a couple of things to do in my room, but I'll be down in a few minutes."

I sprinted up the stairs, closed the door behind me, and tossed my jacket on the bed. Without giving myself time to consider what I was about to do, I pulled the dresser out from the wall just far enough that I could get to the small door. I pulled the door toward me, stooped down, and entered the candy garden for the third time. Disappointment welled up inside me when I saw that the garden had changed from my original impression of it. The sparkly grass was not as bright as before and the trees had lost their red and yellow gumdrop leaves. I wandered down the twisting taffy path and examined the rest of the garden to see if it had changed, too. While the candy bushes had not vanished, the colors were not as brilliant as I recalled from my initial visit. The candy corn weeds had grown taller, and the bed of fudge had expanded and taken over the patch of green and blue buds that the gingerbread man had told me represented my understanding. The green and blue buds, fully opened now, poked up through the fudge and swayed gently in the enchanted air.

This time I was expecting the tiny voice, but my heart still thumped loudly when I heard it. "There you are! I've been waiting for you. Where were you?"

"Hello, Tiny."

"Hello, Sam. If you are looking for the gingerbread man, he won't be back, today. You do realize that he doesn't stay here all the time, don't you? But if you really need him, he'll know. He hung around here frequently in the last few weeks, waiting for you to discover your legacy." The greenish light pulsed brighter. "I miss hearing him swinging through the branches singing his silly songs. I could hear him coming from quite a distance bellowing at the top of his voice, 'She'll be coming 'round the mountain' or 'I've been working on the railroad'. Now that you know that you're a witch, he'll still be here when you need him. He just won't be hanging around your door all the time." The voice held a hint of regret, and I believed that Tiny really would miss the feisty little gingerbread man. Who else would keep her company in her lonely vigil by the small doors? Tiny sighed deeply, "Yes, I will miss him. I enjoyed his company and the stories he told. But enough of that. You didn't come here to hear me reminisce, did you?"

"That's all right. I've decided that I need to listen more to others. People around me lead much more interestin' lives than I ever would have imagined. If I'm gonna make wise use of my new-found powers, then I need to learn all I can from others so I can make good decisions myself." I wandered to the edge of the lemon drop bed and plucked one of the candy corn weeds. I held it up. "What does this plant represent? I remember that Samuel told me the lemon drops were intelligence, but he didn't mention these corn candies. Do you know what they are?"

Tiny's laughter sounded like bells ringing as she answered, "Funny you should ask. Those candy corn plants represent one thing that will take you farther in life than many of the other qualities combined. The candy you are holding, Sam, is your sense of humor. Although this candy garden may change from time to time, the magic and the sense of humor will always be here to help you when the serious business of life becomes too heavy."

"Why has the magic fudge overtaken the understandin' plants?" I continued down the winding path and Tiny tagged along.

"You know that, Sam. Think about it."

"Is it because I now understand that I possess magical powers and have decided to learn how to use them?" I plucked one of the after dinner mints and held it up for Tiny to see, if she could see. "What is this?"

"The after dinner mint represents your honesty and fair play. Honesty is very important, but there will be times when you must lie to protect your secret. Don't feel bad when this happens, there is nothing else you can do. Above all, you need to keep mortals from finding out your secret." Tiny's light flickered. "It is almost time for you to return to your world, Sam. Is there anything else you want to know before you go?"

I turned to look at the altered candy garden. "Will you be here when I come through that door again, or will you disappear like the gingerbread man?"

Tiny's voice seemed to be drifting farther away as she responded, "The gingerbread man did not disappear. He just isn't here at the present time. As for me, I may be here or I may not. I tend to many doors, many worlds, and many secrets. You must go, but I'll leave these words with you:

> *Use your magic sparingly,*
> *Not to impress your friends.*
> *Use your powers wisely,*
> *Or you must make amends.*

"Goodbye for now, Sam. I'll give Samuel your regards when I see him again."

By this time, we had returned to the small door, and as I bent down to re-enter my room, I heard Aunt Kate calling me to lunch.

I didn't really have answers to all the questions that ran through my mind, but I felt better about being a witch. It wouldn't be easy, and I would need to control foolish urges to show off my witchcraft. I would listen to what Mrs. Lawrence had to teach me, and I would do my best to make her proud of me. With renewed determination, I closed the small door into my bedroom, pushed the dresser into place, and went to join my family for lunch.

We had barely seated ourselves at the kitchen table when the phone shrilled.

"I'll get it," I pushed back my chair and crossed the room to the wall phone by the back door. Checking Caller ID, I saw that the call was coming from Carl's house.

"Hello," I said.

"Sam, this is Mrs. Parker. Is Carl with you? I've checked everywhere else, but I can't find him." Her voice sounded all choked-up like she was about to cry. "I didn't call you earlier because I saw you come home alone, but I wondered if maybe Carl told you where he was going. He told me he would be home by eleven thirty, and he's already an hour late."

"Have you tried Mrs. Lawrence's? He told me he was gonna work on his newest invention for a while, and I left him there."

"That's the first place I checked. She said she hasn't seen him since you left and thought he went with you." I could hear the worry in her voice.

I felt my stomach hit bottom as it does when I ride the roller coaster and get to the steep descent. "Don't worry, Mrs. P. I'll call around and see if I can find him." Mrs. Parker hung up, and choking back my own fear, I began calling everywhere where Carl might have gone. I called Ryan's first but no one was home. I checked with Haley, no luck. Desperate, I even called Damien, Darren, Barrett, and Dalton still without success.

I couldn't find Carl anywhere.

18
Green Light

The last place I had seen Carl was in Mrs. Lawrence's basement fiddling around with his invention. Maybe something had gone wrong with the machine, or maybe Carl had somehow locked himself in the basement. I had nothing to lose in checking it myself. "Aunt Kate, can you drive me to Mrs. Lawrence's?"

"That's a good idea, Sam. You should check the last place where you saw him. Of course, I'll drive you to Mrs. Lawrence's or anywhere else you think Carl could be." Aunt Kate grabbed her coat and her car keys as I raced upstairs to get my own jacket. We sprinted toward the car just as a police cruiser with its blue lights flashing pulled up at Carl's house across the street. Carl's mom came running from the house and met the officers halfway down the sidewalk.

"I'll be right back," I called to Aunt Kate as I rushed over to Carl's mom. Mrs. Parker, usually well dressed and well groomed, had buttoned her sweater crooked, and her shoulder length blonde hair looked like she had been running her fingers through it. Tears were running down her face as she turned toward me. "Have you found him, Sam? Is he okay?"

"Not yet, Mrs. P., I'm sorry. But I have one more place to look. I'll call you as soon as I check it out. Do you need Aunt Kate to stay with you until I get back?" I knew that Kate would want to be there to support Carl's mom. Carl's dad was away on a business trip and not due back for another three days.

Aunt Kate had followed me across the street. "Do you want me to stay with you?"

Carl's mom brushed at the fresh tears flowing down her cheeks. "Are you sure you don't mind? I don't want to keep you from anything."

Aunt Kate hesitated and I reassured her that I would be all right. "I don't mind, Aunt Kate. I'll ride my bike over and maybe check out a few other places along the way."

"Be careful, Sam." Kate turned to Carl's mom. "Come on, Sarah, let's go in your house and you can talk to these officers inside." Aunt Kate waved to me, took Mrs. Parker by the arm and led her back into the house, with the two officers following them.

I didn't even wait until the door closed behind them before I ran to the garage and grabbed my bike. I picked up one of the skateboards Carl had left in my garage and placed it in the basket of my bike. If I was right, and Carl was at Mrs. Lawrence's, we could get home faster if we were both on wheels.

Winfield is a small town, and I made it to my great-great grandmother's house in less than ten minutes. Tippy met me on the front porch, and Mrs. Lawrence opened the door before I could ring the bell. It was as if she was expecting me.

I was breathing hard from my ride, and my legs felt shaky. "Mrs. Lawrence, can I check your basement again to see if Carl is there?"

She helped me take my jacket off and tossed it onto one of the chairs in the living room. "I checked the basement after Mrs. Parker called, but it can't hurt to look again."

In the basement, Tippy ran straight to the EATT machine. He lay down facing the door of the machine and laid his huge black head on his extended paws, whining softly.

Mrs. Lawrence and I followed Tippy across the room, and she tried to open the door by pushing some numbers into a number pad that I had failed to see earlier. "I know that's the right combination because Carl had me learn it in case he wasn't here and I needed to use the machine."

She pushed the door but it didn't budge.

I examined the door carefully and discovered a small red light just below the combination pad. I pointed to it. "What does this light mean?"

She punched in the numbers again. "Carl told me he was installing a safety light so that I would know he was inside the machine. He said it would be red if he wasn't there and green if he was. I want to see for myself that this thing is empty." As she entered the final number, the light under the panel flashed from red to green. Suddenly, the invention started humming and the door slowly swung inward.

Carl stepped from the machine. His eyes had a glazed look, and he had to grab the doorframe to keep from falling. Mrs. Lawrence and I rushed forward to catch him as he released his hold and took a hesitant step.

"Carl, what happened? Where've you been? Your mom called the police when you didn't come home, and I've been lookin' for you everywhere." My relief at finding Carl safe mixed with my anger at him for causing his mom and me so much worry.

Mrs. Lawrence stopped my tirade with a small shake of her head as she held onto Carl's right arm and led him toward the stairs. I grabbed his other arm and somehow we got him upstairs and into the living room where we deposited him on the couch.

"Sam, get Carl a glass of water. The glasses are in the cabinet over the sink."

I did as she told me, and when I returned with the water, Carl was sitting on the edge of the couch shaking his head. I handed the glass to Carl and he wasted no time draining it. He returned the glass to me and took a deep breath.

After I placed the empty glass on the coffee table, I sank down on the couch next to Carl and put my arm around his shoulder. "Carl, tell us what happened in the machine."

Carl took another deep breath and shuddered. "I guess I fell asleep," he gasped before his teeth started chattering, and he couldn't speak.

"If you think I believe that, you better think again, Carl, because I know you and I know you haven't taken a nap since we were in Kindergarten. Tell us what really happened and don't leave anything out," I ordered him in my best bossy voice.

Carl laughed shakily. "You're right, as usual, Sam. No, I didn't fall asleep. I was playin' around with those dials on the control panel when I dropped my penknife and it went under the edge of the console. I bent over to pick it up. I remember bumpin' my head and everything went black. The next thing I knew, I was standin' in a small room filled with books on palm readin', werewolves, magic spells, witchcraft, and astrology. I picked up a book about readin' the bumps on people's heads. I don't know the name for it."

Mrs. Lawrence supplied the word Carl was searching for, "Phrenology."

"Yeah, that's it, fernology," Carl agreed. "Anyway, I picked up this book and a slip of paper fluttered out. I picked it up when suddenly I felt a strong suction like someone was usin' a giant vacuum to pull me in. Then I was back in the machine and the rest, you know."

Mrs. Lawrence leaned forward in her chair and peered intently at Carl. "Where is that paper now?"

"I dunno. I guess I dropped it," Carl muttered as he wiped his forehead with the back of his right hand.

I turned to the teacher. "Mrs. Lawrence, do you think it's still in the EATT machine?"

"It could be. We'll go downstairs and check. Before we do, though, there's something you can do for me, Sam." Her eyes met mine as she continued, "Mrs. Lawrence sounds so formal. You can call me Mrs. L. like Carl does."

I tried it out to see how it would sound, "Mrs. L., Mrs. L. It'll take some getting' used to, but I like it."

Mrs. Lawrence stood up and started toward the rear door to the living room. "Now that we have that settled, let's see if we can find Carl's piece of paper." Carl and

I followed the teacher down the stairs and across the basement to the machine.

Through the open door, I could see the chair and a corner of the control panel, but no sheet of paper. Carl stepped into the machine and emerged triumphantly a minute later holding a piece of paper about the size of a three by five index card. "Found it!" he shouted, waving it like a small flag.

Mrs. Lawrence extended her left hand and Carl handed the paper to her. She examined it carefully, even holding it up to the light and peering at it front and back. After finishing her examination, she turned, proffering the paper to me. "I don't see anything on here," she commented. "Perhaps you would like to look at it, Sam." A small smile played at the corner of her lips as she placed the item in my hand.

As the paper touched my skin, I felt a tingling sensation begin at my fingertips and travel up my arm. What did Mrs. L. mean there was no writing on the paper? The words written on the page in faded blue ink were clearly visible to me.

*"Your action and not your intent
Is what others will always see.
You have a gift that can torment
Unless you use it wisely."*

I held the paper up and read the verse aloud. When I had finished, Carl grabbed the paper from my hand and studied the back of the page. He frowned slightly as he shifted his eyes from the page to my face and back again. "There is nothing on this paper," he commented as he returned it to me.

"Sure there is." I held the paper up again and read:

*"No matter what tomorrow brings
Or what the future holds,
Hope eternal in you springs
As each new day unfolds."*

"That's not what you read the first time," Carl insisted. "I know what I heard, and that wasn't it. What kind of joke are you pullin' on us, Sam?"

Mrs. Lawrence motioned for me to hold the paper up and turn it over. I did as she indicated and saw that each side of the page contained a quatrain written in the same faded ink. The ink and the slant of the handwriting looked familiar, and suddenly, I realized that the person who wrote these two verses was the same person who had written the date on Carl's photograph of the town.

Gently, Mrs. Lawrence took the paper from me and held it up once again for Carl to examine. His frown deepened as he gazed at the page. "Why can't I see anythin' on that paper when you or I hold it? Why do the words show up when Sam holds it?"

Mrs. Lawrence put the card in her pocket. "Obviously, Sam possesses a gift that you and I don't have. She has the ability to see what others can't see on paper," she paused. "Or in a photograph." She closed the door to the machine. "Let's go back upstairs and get something to eat." As Mrs. Lawrence once again led the way up the steep stairs, I remembered that I hadn't eaten lunch because I was looking for Carl. I hadn't realized how hungry I was.

As we settled at the kitchen table, it occurred to me that I forgotten to phone Carl's mom to tell her he was safe. "Carl, you need to call your mom and let her know that you're all right. Tell her you'll be home soon. She doesn't need to come get you because I brought one of your old skateboards. And could you tell Aunt Kate I'll be home soon and not to hold lunch for me?"

"Good idea, Sam," Mrs. Lawrence added. "Carl, you can use the phone in the living room to call your mom so she can stop worrying about you. Tell her that you were working on your invention and lost track of the time."

Carl slumped in his chair. "What if she grounds me for makin' her worry?"

Mrs. Lawrence put her hand on his shoulder and said, "If she grounds you, she grounds you, and you'll have to live with it. However, I have a feeling that she will be so glad to know you're fine, that she won't punish you."

Carl smiled his endearing crooked smile and stood reluctantly to go make his call.

While Carl was in the living room, Mrs. Lawrence and I bustled around her kitchen throwing together some ham and cheese sandwiches. When Carl returned, smiling from ear to ear, I knew his mom wasn't going to punish him for scaring her. We devoured the sandwiches as if we hadn't eaten in days. When we finished, Carl pushed his chair back and patted his stomach. "Thanks, Mrs. L. That was delicious."

"You're welcome, Carl. Now tell me. What, if anything, did you learn from today's experience?"

"What did I learn? Well," he paused scratching the back of his neck, "I learned that my mom worries about me when I don't get home on time. I also learned that Sam is a true friend and worries about me, too." Carl laughed as he added, "I guess I also learned that I shouldn't work on my inventions unless someone is around to help me if things go wrong. Just think," he shuddered. "I could still be in that room with those books if you hadn't pulled me back when you entered the code on the panel."

I couldn't resist, "Were you afraid you'd learn somethin' from all those books?"

I could see the muscles at the corners of Mrs. Lawrence's mouth twitch as she tried not to smile. Turning to me she inquired, "Sam, what did you learn?"

I had had some time to think about it, so I had my answer ready. "I learned it's ok to ask questions when you don't understand somethin'." I smiled at my great-great grandmother. "And I learned that everyone has secrets that may or may not be revealed." I placed my hand over Carl's. "Also, none of us knows what will happen in the future, but we gotta make the best of each situation as it comes up."

Carl added, "Yeah, we gotta face the fact that we're different from most people. Our lives will never be the same again, but no matter what happens tomorrow or the next day, life will never be dull."

I stood and took my dishes to the sink. "You're right, Carl. We aren't like everyone else. I have a feelin' that our mundane lives have changed forever, whether we like it or not. But right now, I'm gonna do somethin' completely normal and go shoppin' with Aunt Kate." I grabbed Carl by the hand, pulling him up from his chair. Waving our goodbyes to Mrs. Lawrence, Carl and I stepped out into the cold air just as the first snowflake fell.

Printed in the United States
51336LVS00002B/1-156